BREATH
OF A
GHOST

Acknowledgements:
Special thanks to my sister, Iris Loewen, for her constant
encouragement. Also to Martin Oordt and Blair McMurren,
who read the manuscript and provided many valuable
editorial suggestions, and to my editor, Sheila Dalton, who
did such an incredible job of polishing the final product.

BREATH OF A GHOST

ANITA
HORROCKS

Published in 1996 by
Stoddart Publishing Co. Limited
34 Lesmill Road
Toronto, Canada
M3B 2T6
Tel. (416) 445-3333
Fax (416) 445-5967

Canadian Cataloguing in Publication Data
Horrocks, Anita, 1958–
Breath of a ghost

A JUNIOR GEMINI BOOK

ISBN: 0-7736-7453-5

I. Title.

PS8565.066B7 1996   jC813'.54   C96-930910-4
PZ7.H67Br 1996

Cover Design: Bill Douglas at The Bang
Computer Graphics: Mary Bowness

*Stoddart Publishing gratefully acknowledges the support of the
Canada Council and the Ontario Arts Council in the development
of writing and publishing in Canada.*

Printed and bound in Canada

To Bryan, who never once doubted.

And for Ali, Robin and Erin,
who told me to write a ghost story, cheered me on
and let me know exactly what they thought.

"Like children, you are haunted with a fear that when the soul leaves the body, the wind may really blow her away and scatter her."

— *Socrates, Greek philosopher,*
died 399 B.C.

THE DREAM

I raced through the night with Jeri and Ringo, laughing.

The wind was blowing. It gathered force over the mountains and emptied onto the prairies, melting the first pitiful snowfall of the year with one huge warm sigh for the end of summer.

Jeri and I were dressed like skeletons, black with glowing white bones. Maybe it was Halloween.

Crazy dream. Jeri was dead. He couldn't run anymore. And even before Jeri died, Ringo — our dog — wasn't allowed to be around him. But there we were, howling along with that crazy dog at the full moon staring down at us as if it knew what was coming even if we didn't, and had arranged for the best place in the sky to watch it all happen. Cold silvery light threw shadows across our path and jumped out at us from behind bushes, trying to trip us up.

We left the street and ran across a field. Where the field dropped over the edge of a deep coulee we stopped, laughing hysterically, to catch our breath.

I listened to the broken cries and moans carried on the wind, the sounds of lost souls escaping lifeless bodies. I lifted my face to feel its breath, wondering what past lives floated from the mountains and were touching me now.

Ringo danced and barked in circles around us. Then, just like that, he stopped and looked across the ravine to the ridge on the other side. His ears went straight up and the hair on the back of his neck bristled. He growled deep in his throat. I turned in the direction he was looking and felt the hair on the back of my own neck stand on end.

Suddenly the night was filled with a hollow, tormented howl.

A dark shape stood on the ridge, boldly black against the moon, its pointed nose lifted to the sky. A second furious wail slashed at us through the night air and echoed down the valley.

"It's time to go, Dari." The voice at my side was quiet, weary.

I turned to look at my little brother, Jeremiah. I was holding his hand and he was looking up at me. Except I couldn't see his face, just a pale skull with holes where his eyes should be. "Please, Dari. I'm tired. I want to go now."

I wanted to go, too. Instead I started to scramble down the slope of the coulee towards the dark tangled shadows below. "We can't let it scare us," I said. "Nothing is gonna scare us, right?"

He just stood there, lost, looking like he didn't know where to turn. "I'll wait, Dari. I'll wait here until you come back."

I nodded and started down the slope again.

"Make sure you come back, Dari." The shadows closed and swallowed his tiny voice.

The wind blew.

CHAPTER ONE

I woke up in a cold sweat, Jeri's voice echoing inside my head. "I'll wait, Dari." My sheets and pillow were soaked and I was shaking. I threw off my blankets and sat up to catch my breath.

I knew why I dreamt about Halloween and coyotes howling. Because Halloween was Jeri's birthday. And coyotes always frightened him, just like the wind howling at night frightened him. I wondered if he was still scared now.

I was. It was two months since Jeri had died and I was still having the same nightmare. Almost every morning I woke up soaked in sweat. Almost every morning I lay in bed and listened for the wind.

When I was little, I thought the shriek of the wind was ghosts wailing as they floated across the prairies. The idea was beginning to haunt me again now, even though I was twelve and old enough to know it was only my imagination.

Living in Lethbridge, you eventually get used to the wind or else it drives you crazy. The chinooks come whipping down over the mountains and hit southern Alberta in full force. One time, driving home with my dad from the mall in the spring, the wind was so strong it picked up the sand and gravel left behind after the snow melted and sand-blasted our car. The sound was like a hailstorm. I ducked behind the seat. I thought the windshield was going to break for sure.

When we got to our street corner, we couldn't even see what color the traffic lights were because they were flying straight out, shining up at the sky.

The wind blew like that all week. People just went about their business. Dad got a new windshield, muttered a few curses and that was that. Except I did hear Mom and Dad talking one night about how there were always more accidents and crimes and suicides and weird stuff happening when the wind blew like that.

At least the chinooks are warm, so sometimes the weather is like spring in the middle of winter. And the wind doesn't blow all the time here, like some people think.

But it blew in my nightmares, where it was always late fall, with only a few stubborn leaves left clinging to their lifelines. Cold and icy grey, like my insides.

The ice had been there for so long that I felt like I was starting to freeze from the inside out. I only ever warmed up when I got mad, and then it burned like the time I froze my toes tobogganing. When they started to thaw, sharp pricks of fire shot through my feet.

I was mad a lot these days, but I didn't care. Little brothers were not supposed to get sick and die. That was all there was to it.

I got out of bed and kicked the clothes on the floor out of my way as I headed for the window, putting my nightmare to the back of my mind.

There was no wind. The warm smells and sounds of an early summer morning made their way into my room through the open window. A meadowlark burst into its staccato song and I saw its yellow, black-collared vest puff up. I breathed in the tang of ozone in the fresh-washed air and the green smell of mown grass. All the leaves on the trees were pretty much out now. The Mayday tree in our front yard looked like a huge bouquet of white flowers.

Ringo, in his usual place on the rug beside my bed, lifted his head and watched me walk across the hall and stop in the doorway to Jeri's room. I wondered why Mom left the door open all the time and didn't bother to put away any of Jeri's things, or even change the Sesame Street quilt on his bed. Ringo trotted up beside me. I reached down and scratched behind his ears.

"Morning, Ringo." He looked at me and whined softly. "Yeah, I feel the same way, fella." I smiled at him.

Ringo was all black and white except for lopsided rings of light brown fur around his eyes and down his back legs. One ring spread across his cheek, making him look like a clown or maybe a boxer who had gone one too many rounds.

He followed me to the bathroom and stared at me staring at myself in the mirror. My hair hung in tangled dark brown waves almost to my shoulders and it shocked me to see how sad my eyes looked in my long, thin face. They didn't seem like my eyes somehow. I brushed my teeth because I couldn't stand the scummy taste in my mouth, but didn't bother to brush my hair. Back in my room I pulled on jeans and a t-shirt, jammed my Jays cap over my hair and closed the door on my unmade bed. No one would notice.

No one noticed anything I did these days, except Ringo. He'd been sent to stay with one of my friends after Jeri got sick. But he still whined and sniffed at Jeri's bedroom door like he expected him to come back. Some nights, Ringo scratched at my closed bedroom door until I got up and let him out. Then he trotted across the hall and slept on Jeri's bed. In a way, it felt good to look across the hall and see someone there.

I was glad today was Saturday. No school for two whole days — two whole days in which I didn't have to put up with people staring at me or feeling sorry for me. I wondered what I would do all weekend. I sure didn't plan on doing any homework. And I didn't feel like calling any of my friends, either.

No one else was around when I got downstairs. Mom was probably sleeping late again. She did that a lot since Jeri died. I didn't have a clue where Dad was. But the coffee pot was full, so I figured he wasn't far away.

I decided to grab something to eat and get out of the house before he saw me. I filled Ringo's water dish and helped myself to a bowl of cereal. But I was still sitting at the table munching away when Dad came in from the garage. Too late.

"Morning, Darien." Dad went over to the sink to wash his hands.

"Hi, Dad," I muttered through a mouthful of cereal.

"What are you up to today?" He poured himself a cup of coffee.

I thought fast. I knew where this was heading and I wasn't interested. Lately my dad had been trying to get me to do things with him. I just wanted to be left alone.

"Ringo needs some exercise. And I have a project due on Monday for social studies," I lied. I'd already finished my project.

"I was thinking about cleaning out the garage, maybe taking a few things down to the Salvation Army. Think you might have time to help for a couple of hours? We could stop for a burger or something after."

"Sorry, gotta go." I put my dish in the dishwasher, grabbed an apple off the counter and left him holding his cup of coffee. Ringo trotted out the door after me. As the door closed behind me, I called back over my shoulder, "I'll be home for dinner."

"I thought —," Dad started to call after me.

Yeah, well you thought wrong, Dad. I was already around the corner of the house and gone. I planned to get lost for the rest of the day.

Ringo and I ran across the street.

CHAPTER TWO

In just a couple of minutes Ringo and I were at the edge of the coulees. I headed for the spot where a gentle slope led down to the bottom of the ravine.

We live in a new subdivision just outside Lethbridge. Our street has houses on only one side. Between our neighborhood and the rest of the city is nothing but flat prairie and farmers' fields. Our back yard disappears into a coulee and in front is an empty field that stops short at the top of the river valley before crumpling into more coulees. In the valley along the Oldman River is a huge park, a bunch of parks really, with cycling and hiking trails, picnic areas and a couple of golf courses. One of the golf courses is below our place.

I stayed away from the parks usually. There were too many people. But the steep slopes and deep gullies of the coulees were perfect for climbing and exploring. All kinds of animals and birds lived there. In some places, the slopes are like canyon walls, bare dirt and rocks rising straight up. That's why the golf course is called Canyon Greens. In other places, the slopes aren't as steep and are covered with grass and prairie flowers, including a whole lot of cactus.

I wasn't supposed to go into the coulees alone. Since Jeri died, my mom and dad warned me a hundred times to stay out of them unless I was with someone. They thought I'd twist an ankle and never find my way out, or something. Now that summer was almost here they were worried about snakes. I figured it was just another way for them to tell me what to do, as if they didn't have enough ways already.

I didn't want anyone else around today except Ringo. The coulees were the perfect place to get away from everybody. What Mom and Dad didn't know wouldn't hurt them.

"Let's go, Ringo."

The trail was crossed by deer tracks and was a little slick from yesterday's rain, so I picked my way carefully down the slope while Ringo walked easily along beside me.

It took longer than I thought it would to get to the bottom, because the trail was so slippery. Once there, I scrambled along beside the stream, climbing over rocks and jumping across places where the slope had collapsed because of erosion. At one spot there was a tangle of thorny buffaloberry bushes and wolf willow. I tried pushing my way through, but the bushes were too thick. There was an old wagon in the way, too, turned upside-down in the middle of all the bushes. The wood was half-rotted and the wheels were sticking straight up into the air. Scratched, and choking on the sweet perfume from the bushes' tiny flowers, I decided to leave the briarpatch to the rabbits and climb up the slope instead. I didn't mind the extra effort. Down here, with the steep sides of the ravine towering above me, I was in another world. Nothing that happened on the prairie mattered. I could handle thorny bushes, collapsed slopes and uneven paths.

We were more than halfway to the valley bottom when Ringo gave a sharp bark. He was dancing and sniffing around something lying on the opposite side of the creek. Whatever it was, it wasn't moving, so I jumped across the water to get a closer look.

I wished I hadn't. Lying there, twisted and torn apart, was what was left of a fawn. It wasn't much. A few bits of black flesh hung from the skeleton. Big blue-black flies buzzed around it. Most of the bones were held together in clumps by stiffened pieces of hide. Dried blood darkened the ground under the carcass. There was enough fur left for me to see the light spots that once covered the fawn's coat. Close by was the bottom half of a leg with a tiny hoof. As I watched, a beetle crawled out from inside the broken end.

My legs suddenly felt like they couldn't hold me up and I stumbled a few steps away from the carcass to lean on a rock, waiting for the coulee to stop tilting. A familiar stab shot up my stomach and into my throat.

The fawn was just a baby. The coyotes had probably got it. Down here, if something wasn't strong enough to look after itself, it wasn't going to survive.

My mouth was dry and I wished I'd remembered to bring my water bottle. Next time, I'd make sure I was ready to spend the whole day out here. I'd left in such a hurry I hadn't even brought a sandwich. I felt in my pocket for the apple, but it was early yet. Better to save it for later.

I caught a whiff of the carcass starting to stink in the heat, and turned away so I wouldn't gag. The warm morning was turning into a hot summer day as the sun climbed overhead. There wasn't even a hint of a breeze. When I got to the river, though, I would be able to cool off in the water.

I got up and started walking again. It seemed like a long time before I finally reached the river valley. The coulee slopes fell away and the fourth green of the golf course lay spread out in front of me like a welcome mat. Two bright blue splashes of color flicked across it and I watched until the pair of bluebirds landed in some bushes on the other side. If I followed the bluebirds around the green, I could disappear into the narrow band of woods along the river.

I decided to take the direct route instead, over a small ridge beside the green. Once over the top, there was just a pile of rocks between me and the river. The flowing water looked clear and cold, running over a bed of smooth stones. I felt cooler already.

Ringo chose that moment to start acting up. He didn't follow me when I started to pick my way down the rocks. He stood at the top of the rock pile, barking. I couldn't believe that he picked now to get stubborn.

"I'm going to the river, Ringo. You don't want to come, that's fine by me."

There was a huge flat rock almost at the

bottom where I could soak up the sun for a while after a dip in the water. I was almost there when the uneasy feeling I'd had since seeing the fawn began to grow.

I stopped and looked around. Eyes. I felt eyes on me. Someone was there, watching me, I was sure of it. Even though it was quiet, and I didn't see anyone, I couldn't shake the feeling that someone was there.

"Ringo! Come here, boy." He just barked at me. "Come here, Ringo," I commanded.

He didn't like it, but he made his way down to me. I hung onto his collar in case whatever was around made him take off. Maybe there was a golfer trying to fish a bad shot out of the river. I could just make out the voices of some golfers on the green behind the ridge. But there was no one in sight.

It was weird. The feeling of being watched was so strong, I felt if I reached out I could touch whoever it was. Yeah, right, I thought. I'm not only having crazy dreams, now I'm beginning to act crazy, too. But I sure wasn't prepared for what happened next.

I took a step toward the flat rock and, just like that, the feeling of being watched turned into panic. I couldn't move my feet. My heart thumped in my throat, and I whipped my head around. I felt the warning just as clearly as if someone had shouted, "Run!"

Then a breath of chill air floated by my face. It smelled familiar, not bad but somehow out of place. I took a deep breath, trying to slow my thumping heart and figure out what the smell was. I almost felt I knew it, and then the cold breath turned into a steady stream of air that wound its way around me, circling my body, lower and lower. I was still holding onto Ringo with one hand, which was a good thing because suddenly I was pushed backwards as though a huge gust of wind caught me off balance. Except this wasn't a gust at all but more like someone pushing me. I felt myself falling.

"What the —?"

Only the stream of air around me kept me from toppling over the rocks. I moved back with it and dragged Ringo along. A few steps and the chill was gone as suddenly as it had appeared. I was back in the warm sunshine.

Okay, I thought, take it easy. Just take it easy. Hearing, seeing, smelling things. It's all part of going crazy. I'd hardly swallowed the terrible taste in my mouth before Ringo started to bark furiously, growling and pulling to be let go. But I wasn't letting go, not when I saw what he was barking at.

From under a ledge overhanging the flat rock, a huge snake wound its way into the sunlight. There were blotchy brown markings on its grey-brown skin and a rattle at the end of its tail.

The snake coiled itself upright in the middle of the rock and lifted its head high in the air. Its tongue flicked out at me and its tail rattled. Another snake followed and then another. I looked down into the crevice beside the rock and saw hundreds of writhing shapes twisting their way up to the sunlight, hissing and rattling.

That was enough for me. I held tight onto

Ringo's collar and dragged him back up the ridge. I forgot all about wading in the river, and didn't let go of Ringo until we were back on our street, in case he got any dumb ideas about going rattler hunting. The haunting sense of someone beside me stayed with me as we went, and every once in a while I felt a cool breath drift across my face. The air felt good against my hot skin and helped calm me.

I looked back once, just before I turned toward home. And that was when I saw the coyote.

It stood on the top of the ridge, scraggy and huge, watching me from the other side of the coulee. Just like in my dream. That's when the cool breath quivered across my face and was gone.

I couldn't move. Sure, there were plenty of coyotes around. I knew that. But this coyote was different. I could feel its anger all the way across the coulee, and I staggered. Then it turned and casually, carelessly, disappeared behind the ridge.

My mind was numb, so my legs took over.

They walked me into the house and upstairs to my bedroom without me even thinking about Mom or Dad seeing me. Shaking, I closed the door, sat down on the bed and hugged Ringo hard.

Then I realized it wasn't so much the snakes or even the coyote that was frightening me. It was the cold stream of air that pushed me away from the snakes, that stayed with me all the way back to the prairie, that trembled and fled when the coyote appeared.

I was shaking because of the breath that touched my face and smelled just like Jeri.

CHAPTER THREE

It was the smell of that cool breath that started me remembering things I usually tried not to think about. I closed my eyes and saw Jeri hit me with a flying tackle, just like it was happening right then instead of last fall.

I'd been on my way home from a soccer game when Jeri had tackled me. We'd rolled across the lawn until I was on my back with Jeri on top of me. Ringo bounced in circles around us, darting in here and there with an encouraging nip.

"Gotcha!" Jeri raised his arms above his

head in victory and then the next second, wrinkled his nose and jumped up. "You stink!"

I lifted my arm and took a whiff. "Just dirt and sweat. Soccer's a sweaty game." I let him pull me up and we went inside. I shook off my cleats at the back door. They stank worse than me.

"Didja win?" asked Jeri.

"Of course. Where were you?"

"Mom and me went shoppin'! Look!" He turned around so I could see the miniature purple backpack he was wearing. "It's for school. To carry my stuff."

"Cool. What else did you get?"

"I got new crayons and glue and a sticker book. And we gots you lots of stuff, too."

I groaned. "Thanks for reminding me that school starts next week."

"Yeah." Jeri let the word linger on his mouth.

School was like a dream come true for him. But I figured he'd clue in before long. He was pretty smart for an almost five-year-old just starting kindergarten. I was going into grade six so it wasn't as bad as I made out. I was almost looking forward to me and my friends having the run of the school.

I filled Ringo's water dish and opened the fridge door. "What did Mom buy for snacks?"

"Peanut butter!"

Sometimes I swore Jeri lived on peanut butter. Peanut butter on his toast at breakfast, peanut butter cookies for snacks, peanut butter "samwitches" for lunch. One time when Dad barbecued steaks for supper, Jeri gave his to Ringo so he could have a peanut butter sandwich instead.

"Talk about stink, peanut butter breath."

He held his hand up in front of his mouth and blew, then took a giant whiff. He grinned at me. "Yep!"

On the first day of preschool, he packed enough peanut butter sandwiches into his backpack to feed the whole class. Mom tried to tell him she would pick him up before lunch, but he didn't care. He just stood on a chair by the counter and spread the stuff on the bread thicker.

"Maybe I'll be hungry before you come get me."

When I got home that day, Jeri was waiting for me.

"We had snack time and I ate my peanut butter samwitch. And Robert had one and Cory had one and Amy had one. T'morrow I'm gonna bring one for Brook, too."

"Who's Brook?" I teased. "Is she your girlfriend?"

He nodded. "I'm gonna ask her. She called me Jer-ee-my-ah. Look!" He stuck his elbow out at me. A Big Bird bandaid was stuck over a juicy red raspberry scrape that spread from his elbow halfway to his wrist. "I went swoosh down the slide. Like this. So fast." He showed me how fast by sliding across the kitchen floor.

Ringo wanted to play too. He clamped his mouth over Jeri's sneaker and tried to drag him across the floor.

"And I hit right here." Jeri stuck his elbow in the air and pointed. "Let go, Ringo." He shook his foot free.

I inspected his battle wound. "Yep. I'd say

that was a first-class injury. Maybe Mom will let you stay home from school tomorrow."

He shook his head. "Uh-uh. No way. It'll be all gone t'morrow."

It wasn't, of course, but it was only a scrape and he still went to preschool the next day and the next. The fourth day, though, he came home with a sore throat and by the next morning he had a temperature. Mom bundled him up in bed.

He spent all that weekend in bed. His nose ran and his eyes watered and his throat was so sore he wouldn't even eat peanut butter sandwiches. He was better on Monday, but still not well enough to go to school. By the middle of the week, he started to get grumpy.

I'd never seen him in a bad mood before. Jeri always smiled. As soon as he woke up in the morning, his face broke into this big grin and his eyes lit up. Some of my friends complained about their little brothers and sisters, but I never did. Jeri made me laugh.

Except now he wasn't happy at all. Even after being in bed all day he was tired. "My legs hurt me, Dari. I don't want to eat."

It wasn't like Jeri to complain and that worried me a little. Still, Mom and Dad thought it would be good for him to come downstairs and eat at the table, so I tried bribing him.

"Okay, peanut butter breath. How about a piggyback ride?"

He didn't scramble up like usual, but stood up on the bed slowly and reached out his arms. I started to turn around so he could climb on my back when I noticed the sleeve of his pyjamas was red.

"What'd you do? Bump your elbow again?" I pulled up the sleeve and looked at the scrape that was more than a week old now. Blood had soaked right through the bandaid, obliterating Big Bird. Jeri twisted around to look and gave a loud protest when I stripped off the bandaid.

"Ow! It's not gone yet, Dari."

"I'll get you a new one." We stopped in the bathroom and I cleaned his elbow and slapped a new bandaid on it. Then we headed downstairs.

"Jeri's elbow still isn't better," I told Mom and Dad as we sat down to dinner. "Shouldn't it have stopped bleeding by now?"

Jeri stuck his elbow up obligingly so Mom could see the blood seeping through the bandaid.

"I'm taking him to the doctor tomorrow," said Mom. "He's been sick a whole week now with this cold. I'll have him look at the elbow, too."

"I want to go to school," Jeri said.

Mom smiled at him. "We know, honey. After you go to the doctor I'm sure you'll be back in school in no time."

But he wasn't. The doctor looked him over and scheduled some tests for the next day. Jeri never came home that night. Neither did my mom.

It was a Friday. I was helping myself to a snack after school when Dad came home early to pack up some of Jeri's stuff. He told me Jeri had to stay in the hospital and Mom was going to spend the night with him. That was it. Nothing about what was wrong with him. I was so stunned, I forgot to ask.

"Here," I said, handing him Jeri's purple backpack as he went out the door. "Don't forget this."

I made peanut butter sandwiches for my dinner after he left. Ringo and I ate alone.

CHAPTER FOUR

I heard a door slam outside and shook my head, trying to stop the memories, wishing I could shut them off like a movie on the VCR. But the pictures kept coming like I'd pushed fast forward instead. And they not only had color and sound but smells, too. I closed my eyes and took a deep breath and could actually smell Jeri's breath, the cool, minty-clean toothpaste scent and underneath, the warm, peanutty richness.

Lots of nights, especially when the wind blew or the coyotes howled at the moon, Jeri would sneak across the hall from his bedroom and crawl into bed with me. He'd curl up in a tight ball beside me and his soft breath would drift across my face. Peanut butter and toothpaste breath. The toothpaste never quite got rid of the peanut butter part. Jeri would sleep like a rock and I'd dream about swimming in huge vats of melted peanut butter.

I opened my eyes and blinked hard to stop the memories. Jeri was dead now. Had been for two months. But I'd smelled his breath today by the river.

I forced myself to think again about what had happened in the coulee. Someone or something had been watching me. I'd felt it by the rocks before I saw the snakes. And whatever it was, it tried to warn me. It stayed close by, until the coyote came. Whatever it was with me there in the ravine didn't like that coyote any more than I did.

But *nothing* was there. I just imagined it. It was a warm day and I'd started day-dreaming and imagined the whole thing. The wind simply gusted and caught me off balance so that I fell back.

Except there was no wind today. And I never knew any wind to smell like peanut butter and toothpaste before.

I went to the window and leaned out. There was nothing in the air but the same hint of yesterday's rain that I'd smelled that morning, carried on a warm breeze I could barely feel. But then it wasn't unusual for the wind to come and go as it pleased around here.

And there was nothing unusual about seeing a coyote on the prairie, either. This one just happened to show up there while I was still upset from seeing the snakes.

I sighed and lay back on my bed. Ringo jumped up beside me and I reached over to pull him close. The house was silent, but I was used to that. Mom slept almost all the time, or at least stayed in her room, and my friends hardly ever called anymore. After Jeri got sick, I spent most of my free time with him when he was home. And when he was in the hospital, I kept to myself, because I wanted it that way.

Brad and Ryan and a few of my other

friends came to Jeri's funeral just before Easter. Afterwards, I didn't much feel like being around anyone, and they could take a hint. My birthday was a few weeks after Jeri died, but I didn't have a party. It didn't feel right for me to play and have fun when Jeri would never play again. Turning twelve didn't feel like anything to celebrate.

Ringo whined and I unwrapped my arms from his neck to scratch behind his ears. "Sorry, fella." It was only the middle of the afternoon. Too early to make an appearance downstairs. I curled up on top of the bed and fell asleep.

When I woke up, I heard Mom and Dad moving around in the kitchen, and smelled chili. My stomach grumbled, reminding me that I hadn't fed it lunch today. I splashed some water on my face and went downstairs.

"Mmm." Dad's face hovered over the pot on the stove. "I knew the tantalizing aroma of my chilly chili would lure you down sooner or later. Want to know what's in it?"

Dad usually made chili by throwing in every "chilly" leftover he could find in the fridge and then covering it all up with canned tomatoes and a whole pile of chili powder and tabasco sauce. When he got a really potent batch going, just a whiff of the stuff made my eyes water.

"I don't think so."

"Ah, another one who prefers the blind taste test. Alright then, since we're all here, we can chow down."

I watched Mom's eyes flick over to the empty place beside mine. Nice going Dad, I thought. I shot him my best glare and sat at the kitchen table across from Mom. For someone who slept all day, she sure looked tired. There were dark bags under her eyes and her face was pale.

Dad dished out bowls of chili and kept right on trying to get Mom and me involved in his conversation. "Did you get your school work done?"

I shook my head and muttered through a full mouth. "I'll have to finish it tomorrow." That should give me an excuse to get out of whatever Dad planned for Sunday. I just wanted to be alone.

"Mom and I were talking about taking a drive to the mountains. Thought maybe you'd join us."

"Thanks. But I have this project."

Mom still hadn't said anything. I realized we hadn't spoken to each other all day. "Did you show any houses today, Mom?"

I thought that was more tactful than asking straight out if she was ever going to go back to work, which was what I really wanted to know. When Jeri got sick, she took a leave from her real estate job and got another agent to take over her clients.

She looked at me for the first time since we sat down to eat. "Show houses? No. Not today."

"So when?" I asked. This time I ignored my dad's glare.

"I haven't thought about it." Mom got up and started clearing the dishes. "Soon, I suppose."

"It might be good for you to get back to work," Dad added.

She just stared at him. I could see another storm brewing in that look. There'd been enough of them since Jeri died.

"Don't tell me what's good for me." Her voice was hard, and Dad winced.

"I'm not, honey. I just think —" He didn't finish what he was going to say because Mom turned around and left the room.

Dad and I did dishes without saying a word to each other, then we sat around watching TV. Six months before, there was no way I would have been caught dead sitting at home with my parents on a Saturday night. I'd have been at a movie with friends, hanging out playing video games with Brad and Ryan or something. Anything but stay home.

Mom and Dad didn't notice I never had friends around anymore. Mom was in space and Dad was too busy trying to coax her down. I thought about telling them what happened in the coulee, but I knew they'd just get mad at me for going down there alone. Of course, they didn't bother to ask what I'd been doing all day.

They probably wouldn't believe that I saw and felt and even smelled things that weren't there anyway, so why should I bother to tell them?

That night, I had another dream. Jeri was a fawn running down the coulees. The black shadow of the coyote chased him while I stood and watched. I woke up just before the shadow caught him, and lay in bed listening to the coyotes howl in the dark outside my window.

CHAPTER FIVE

On Sunday it rained some more. Mom and
Dad went for a drive anyway. I stayed in my
room and pretended to do homework. I
went down for dinner, then I took Ringo for
a walk. We stayed on the street.

I went back to school Monday without
saying anything about the dead fawn or the
snakes or the coyote in my dream or the cold
breath that blew when there was no wind.

School was one of my least favorite places
since the funeral. Everybody looked at me as
if they felt sorry for me. No one talked about
Jeri or the funeral or even asked what

happened. But there was lots of whispering that ended when I came into a room.

Everyone could quit feeling sorry for me, as far as I was concerned. I didn't need their sympathy and I didn't need them. At least school would be over soon.

But first I had to get through the next couple of weeks. I wheeled my bike into the parking lot and coasted to a stop in front of the bike rack. Brad Reidon and Ryan Cooper walked over to me just as I snapped the lock shut on the rear wheel.

"Hi, Darien," said Brad. "Tried to call you Saturday but your dad said you were out."

"Yeah. Went hiking in the coulees." I felt like I had to explain and that made me mad.

"We had soccer practice and then hung around the mall," Ryan said. "Are you gonna play this year? There's still time to sign up."

Ryan and I were on the same team last year. We'd finished second in our house league. One of the rep team coaches had called and asked us if we wanted to try out for his team this year. Ryan and Brad both tried out and made it.

I might have made the rep team too, but I didn't try out. Things were different now. Soccer belonged in another life. A life in which Jeri and I wrestled in the grass and he told me I stank.

"Don't think so," I answered Ryan. "My parents need me around home." Yeah, right, I thought, after the words popped out of my mouth. Like Mom and Dad know I exist.

"Oh," said Ryan. "Well . . . "

I was saved by the warning bell. "Gotta go. See you guys later."

I joined the stream of kids pushing through the doors. I dumped my jacket and lunch in my locker and made it to homeroom just as the final bell rang. Then I remembered that I had gym first thing. Great, I thought. I forgot to bring my gym clothes. It's gonna be a terrific day.

Gym went okay, though. The teacher, Mr. Whyten, started to show us soccer skills, so we went outside and I could get by with my street runners. I didn't play hard enough to work up a sweat.

After gym I sat through the next two

classes without knowing what they were. My feet just went where they were supposed to go while my brain kept thinking about what'd happened in the coulees.

Language arts, which used to be my favorite class, was just before lunch break. The class had barely started when I got a message to go to the office.

I looked at Mrs. Preston and she nodded. "Go ahead, Darien. You can catch up when you get back."

I got up and walked out, twenty-eight pairs of eyes on my back.

When I got to the office, the guidance counselor was waiting for me. Mr. Stevens wasn't a bad guy, for a teacher. I liked to torment my teachers once in a while with little things like breaking every piece of chalk in the classroom into tiny bits. Even when the other teachers blew up, Stevens never took things too seriously. His punishments were creative, but fair.

"Come on in, Darien." Mr. Stevens waited until I was in his office and then he shut the door behind me. "I'm glad to see there have been no more unscheduled fire drills."

The month before, I'd pulled a fire alarm and cleared the whole school for most of the afternoon. I just couldn't stand to sit in class anymore with everyone staring at me. The unexpected fire drill gave them something else to talk about and besides, I figured it was good practice for everybody.

Stevens talked the Fire Department out of pressing charges even though I didn't tell him why I'd done it. He made me give fire safety lessons to the grade one and two classes for three weeks.

Mom and Dad didn't seem to care. They just signed the paper I put in front of them without saying a thing.

I shrugged at Stevens.

"Sit down." He gestured to the chair facing his desk.

I sat. He sat down too, on the front edge of his desk with one foot on the floor.

"What did I do?" I asked.

He laughed. "Nothing, Darien. Don't worry. I just wanted to see how you were getting along these days."

How I was getting along? Ask my teachers, I felt like saying. But I didn't, of course. The quickest way to get out of here was to answer his questions.

"I'm fine."

Stevens got down to business. "It's been what, just over a month since your brother passed away?"

"Since he died. Yeah. Almost two months." What was this passed away crap? He was dead.

"Your teachers are concerned about you. We know how difficult things must be. Is there anything we can do to help?"

"No, I'm fine. Thanks anyway."

But Stevens wasn't going to let me get away that easily. "How are your parents doing?"

Geez, I thought. Even in school, people worried about my parents.

"They're okay. We miss him and everything. But we're okay, really."

He leaned forward and put a hand on my shoulder. "It's alright, you know, to let people help you. It makes it easier to handle things sometimes if you can talk about them."

"I told you, I'm fine," I repeated. But for some reason, the guy's hand on my shoulder made me feel not so fine. My eyes started to fill up with tears and I blinked them back quickly. "Can I go now?"

"If that's what you want, Darien." His voice was quiet, like he was disappointed. "If you ever need to talk about anything, I'm here."

"Sure." I got up and walked to the door. I wanted to get out of there.

"I have a meeting to go to," he said. "You can stay here until you feel like going back to class."

I was already out the door. The words barely reached me, so they were easy to ignore.

No way was I going back to class. Not with my eyes full of tears and my nose sniffling. I walked right out of the school and over to my bike. I fumbled with my bike lock for a while because my eyes were still swimming. Then it clicked open and I was gone. If I never went back to school again, it would be too soon.

I rode my bike back home and right past our house. There was a trail at the end of the street that led off across the coulees. I followed it along the top of the ridge until I reached the end where the cliff dropped straight down to the valley.

CHAPTER SIX

I sat there at the edge of the coulee ridge and looked down at the river and the valley. Now that I was alone, all the things that'd started pushing their way into my head when Mr. Stevens put his hand on my shoulder came flooding forward.

I remembered knowing that something was wrong with Jeri, but never thinking he might die. Five-year-olds weren't supposed to die. Even when he stayed at the hospital for three weeks, I never once thought he might die.

Mom was hardly home the whole time.

She spent all day with Jeri. Every afternoon, Dad came home from the university where he taught, ate something with me and then went to the hospital to be with Mom and Jeri. They usually didn't get home until after I was in bed.

At first the empty house didn't bother me much. I was busy with soccer and homework and everything else. I went to see Jeri a couple of times, but he seemed okay, just a little tired, and so I didn't worry about him. I kept thinking he'd be home any day.

Before long it was the last week of September, Jeri was still in the hospital and I was playing in the soccer championships. In our league, we played regular games in the spring before school let out, then took a break during summer holidays and started playoffs in September. I rode home after the semi-final game on Saturday and burst into the house to tell Mom and Dad the news.

"We won!" The back door slammed behind me.

There was no answer. Just Ringo, standing in the kitchen and barking a welcome. I forgot everyone was at the hospital.

I left a note on the kitchen table, changed my clothes and rode my bike over to Ryan's. The team was having a party at his place to get psyched for the big game the next day. The coach made sure we all went home early to get a good night's sleep. I was back at my place by nine.

My note was still on the table where I left it and no one was around. I watched TV with Ringo until I heard the car pull up. It was after ten. It ticked me off that they were so late getting home when I had big news to share.

But they were here now, coming in the front door. I jumped up. "We won!"

They smiled. "That's great," said Dad.

"How's Jeri?" I remembered to ask.

"He's doing a little better. If he's still better tomorrow, he'll probably come home this week."

"Alright!" Things looked good all around.

"He asked for you," Mom said. "We told him you were playing soccer."

"That's great he's coming home. He's

okay then, right?" When were they going to ask about the game? "I scored once and Ryan scored twice and we play in the final tomorrow."

"We need to talk to you about that, Darien," said Dad. About what? The game? But why were they acting so strange and serious?

We sat down in the family room. Ringo stretched himself across my lap.

"Jeri has leukemia," Dad said. Just like that.

I didn't understand. "I thought you said he was better. I thought he just had a bad cold and flu."

"He did have a bad cold and flu. But the reason it was so bad is because the leukemia makes it hard for him to get well. They gave him drugs at the hospital to help fight the infections."

Something clicked in the back of my head. "Is that why his sore elbow bled so much?"

"Yes. Because his blood isn't working right. Leukemia is a kind of cancer, Darien. It affects the bone marrow which is where blood cells are made. The cancer cells prevent the bone marrow from making normal blood cells."

I didn't say anything. Jeri had a cancer called leukemia. People who had cancer died. I felt like someone had kicked me in the stomach with a soccer cleat and I couldn't breathe. After a minute, Dad started talking again. I listened carefully.

"Jeri's blood doesn't have enough normal cells. That's why he's tired a lot and sometimes bleeds easily like the way he bled from that scrape."

"We should have told you sooner," Mom added. "We were hoping . . . the tests and the treatments and everything . . . we're sorry, Darien, for not telling you sooner."

"But if he's coming home, he must be better now." I didn't want to hear anymore. "You said he was better."

"He is better, but he's not well. He'll have to go to the hospital every week to continue treatments and have his blood tested to make sure things are okay. He won't be strong enough to play much or go back to preschool. Not yet." Dad stopped and looked straight at me. "There's something you have to do to help him get well."

I noticed he didn't ask me if I'd do whatever it was. He was telling me I had to do it. Of course I'd do whatever I could to help Jeri, so why make it sound like I wouldn't want to?

"Other people can't catch leukemia from Jeri, but he can get sick from our germs. So we'll have to be careful around him and make sure he doesn't catch a cold or anything."

"Okay. No problem." Somehow I got the feeling he wasn't finished.

"It's too risky for children with leukemia like Jeri's to be around pets, Darien. Tomorrow you'll have to find someone to take care of Ringo until Jeri is completely well again."

I scratched under Ringo's white chin and behind his ears. He licked my face. My voice came out a whisper. "It's not fair."

"No. It's not fair," Dad agreed. "But it's not fair for Jeri to have leukemia either."

He was right. I didn't want to do anything that would make Jeri sicker. But I sure was going to miss Ringo. I looked at Mom and Dad. Mom's eyes were red and swollen and tears poured down her cheeks. Dad's eyes were bright, but he wasn't crying. He just looked at me.

I looked back at him.

"Okay," I said.

The next day we lost the championship game by one goal. After the game, I asked Brad if he would look after Ringo and we went to talk to his parents. I explained about Jeri being sick and that I would supply dog food and come over every day to take Ringo for a walk. They said of course Ringo could stay with them. Brad's mom hugged me which made me feel really lousy. Even though I played soccer that day and was sore and tired, I ran all the way home from Brad's.

The next day, Mom and Dad brought Jeri home from the hospital.

CHAPTER SEVEN

Sending Ringo away was tough, I thought. I was still sitting on the coulee ridge remembering things I'd rather forget. Then I heard a shout. I turned. A couple of kids on bikes were racing through the prairie behind me. School must be out. They were shouting at each other, not me.

I couldn't sit in the coulees all night. If anyone saw me now they'd think I was on my way home from school. I wished Ringo was with me. We'd disappear into the coulees where nothing could follow us. We'd run and hide someplace where all these memories couldn't find me. Where I could get things straight in my head again.

And then I saw the trail. It was just another narrow track made by the deer, but this one dropped almost straight down from the top of the ridge to the golf course below. It ended at one of the packed dirt roads used by the golf course maintenance crew. The trail was steep, but I was sure I could make it.

I stood up and yanked my bike upright. It was a mountain bike and made for just this kind of trail. Before I could change my mind, I hopped on and pointed it down the slope.

The first part was easy. I bounced along, touching the brakes just a couple of times. Then I had to brake hard and yank the wheel around, almost do a wheely, to make a turn that cut back down the slope.

After that, it was all I could do to hang on. I picked up speed so fast I knew if I touched the brakes I'd take off right over the handlebars. I had to ride it out and just try to stay on. I was flying. The wind in my face and against my body was the only thing that slowed me down.

Then it happened. I hit a rock and jerked wildly off to the side. The wheels landed sideways with a thump and my elbow scraped against the slope that tilted up to meet me. But soon I was upright again and speeding even faster down the hill.

And someone was with me. I felt it. In the middle of the warm wind rushing into my face was a cooler stream of air. And a familiar smell.

I was almost to the bottom. There was the maintenance road ahead of me. When I reached that, I'd be able to put the brakes on and slow to a stop. I was so busy trying to hang on, I forgot about the cool stream of air. Just had to hang on a little longer.

I didn't have a little longer. A white pickup truck came barrelling around the corner and down the road, heading straight for me. If I didn't stop, I'd be roadkill. There was only one thing I could do. I turned the wheel uphill, straight toward a pile of rocks, squeezed both brakes as hard as I could and closed my eyes.

It wasn't so bad. I even slowed down a

little before the wheels of my bike hit something hard and I nosedived straight over the handlebars. I remembered to tuck and roll, and that may have saved me from breaking any bones. And the ground felt strangely soft, almost like a cushion of air underneath me — until I stopped tumbling and slammed up against a rock. I lay there in a heap, trying to breathe and then trying not to breathe because when I did it was like slamming into the rock all over again.

I heard the truck squeal to a stop and footsteps run up to me. When I opened my eyes, two guys with pale faces were kneeling beside me. "Are you okay, kid?"

Stupid question. I tried to sit up and the sky started to spin. "Bad idea," I said. I put my head down again.

"I'll say. What the hell were you doing riding a bike down that coulee?"

I didn't say anything. There was nothing to say. The trail was there. I was there. "Give me a minute, okay?"

After a while the world stood still again and I lifted my head more cautiously.

"I'm not sure you should try to move," one of the guys said. "Maybe we'd better get help."

"I'm fine. Really. Just a little scraped up."

That was an understatement. When I finally got to a sitting position, I saw just how scraped up I was. My jeans were torn from above one knee down to my ankle. Underneath the tear, my leg was raw. My hand came away sticky-red from my shoulder and I felt the blood trickling down my back. My side throbbed and my face was numb. I didn't want to think about what I looked like. When I tried to stand up, a bolt of lightening shot from my ankle all the way up my leg.

The guys who almost ran me over loaded my twisted bike into the back of their truck and gave me a ride home. They wanted to come in to make sure I was alright, but I talked them out of it.

"Really. I'm fine. My mom's home."

She probably was, too, I thought, as I limped across the driveway and in the back door. She was probably in her room lying down and I wasn't going to let her see me like this. I headed off Ringo's welcoming bark with a sharp command to "Sit!" and a quick pat. "Quiet, boy." Then I hobbled up the stairs as quietly as I could and managed to get myself into the bathroom, Ringo trotting along behind me.

I filled the tub, pulled off my torn clothes and forced myself into the lukewarm water. I tried my best to ignore the stinging and the streaks of red that floated all around me.

I soaked until the stinging stopped and then used a washcloth to clean my leg and as much of my shoulder as I could reach. When I dried off, most of the bleeding had stopped. There was a bottle of alcohol in the medicine cabinet. I used some of Mom's cotton balls to douse the stuff over the scrapes and cuts. Those stings I couldn't ignore. It was all I could do to keep from swearing out loud. Even Ringo whimpered, watching me.

"Yeah, Ringo. It hurts." He whined and backed into the corner.

Not until I'd cleaned the rest of me up as best I could, did I look in the mirror at my

face. And breathed a sigh of relief. The raspberry that stretched from above my right ear
and down to my jaw was a good one alright,
and that side of my face was hot and
swollen. My skin felt scoured. But the scrape
wasn't deep and the bleeding had stopped.
Once I sponged it off with the washcloth,
my face didn't look so bad.

It didn't look so good either. If I was
looking for attention, I was going to get it.
Even Mom and Dad would notice what a
mess I'd made of myself.

My ankle was throbbing, so I limped
across to my room and put on a pair of
shorts and the baggiest t-shirt I could find. I
made my way downstairs with the help of
the railing and found a bag of frozen peas in
the freezer.

It took me a while to find a way to lie on
the sofa without touching any of my scrapes
and bruises. I finally twisted myself onto my
left side with my right foot propped up on a
cushion and resting on the bag of peas.
Ringo contented himself with lying on the
floor beside me.

We were both lying there when Dad walked in the door from work. Mom came down the stairs about the same time. I closed my eyes and waited for the yelling to start.

The room was quiet. I opened my eyes and saw Mom and Dad both looking at my face. Then Mom came over and helped me sit up so she could look at my back and arm. She felt around my ankle, so gently I didn't even wince.

I felt lousy for making them worry but, all the same, it was the first time since Jeri's funeral that Mom had done more than glance at me. Her warm hands felt sort of good. I trembled a little. I didn't want her to stop. I wanted her to put her arms around me and hold me. And then she did.

"I better take him to emergency to have that ankle checked." Dad's voice was tight.

"We'll both go," Mom said, which surprised me again. She brushed my long hair out of my eyes.

At the hospital, they x-rayed my ankle, chest and shoulder and gave me a tetanus shot along with a lecture about doing stupid stunts on bikes. My ankle was sprained, not broken, which I thought it would be by the time the doctor finished twisting and poking at it. It'd swelled up pretty good and was already bruised. The doctor wrapped a tensor around it and told me to keep it iced and stay off it for a day or two. A couple of my ribs had hairline cracks. He taped them up, but said I'd just have to put up with the soreness until they healed.

We were home and I was back on the sofa with frozen peas on my ankle before Dad finally said, "Maybe you should tell us what happened."

So I told them about finding the trail and thinking I could ride my bike down it and how I would have made it if the maintenance truck hadn't come along when it did. I didn't say anything about Mr. Stevens talking to me, or ditching school.

They listened and didn't say much at first. Dad went out to see what my bike looked like.

"Not a very smart thing to try," he said

when he came back. "The bike is pretty much wrecked." He paused and looked puzzled. "You were lucky."

I nodded. There wasn't anything I could say.

"Darien, you have to promise us you'll not do anything like this again." Mom hadn't taken her eyes off me the whole time I was explaining, and now they were shining with tears. "Promise."

"Okay. I'm sorry, really. I'll be more careful." I couldn't stand to see her upset like that.

"You'd better stay home for a day or two," she added. "I'll call the school tomorrow."

"Uhh." I figured I'd better tell them the rest before she found out from Mr. Stevens.

"What?" Mom waited.

"I sort of wasn't in school this afternoon. I was killing time in the coulees when I found the trail."

They looked at me again and I felt real uncomfortable. I would have squirmed if I could. The silence felt worse than any yelling.

Dad said softly, "Seems like you were trying to do more than kill time." What did he mean by that?

They left me watching TV and went into the kitchen. They talked for a long time while Mom made dinner. For the first time in months they didn't argue.

Later that night, Dad helped me up the stairs to bed and both of them came into my room to say good night. I got another flashback of the way things used to be. I didn't hold much hope, though. Jeri was part of how things used to be, and the hole he left was huge.

I tried to find a way to lie on the bed without hurting myself. No such luck. Finally I gave up and settled for the least painful position, on my left side.

In my dreams that night, the dark shadow of the coyote stood high on a ridge. It watched as Jeri and I ran, laughing, up to the edge of the coulee. Jeri stopped while I nose-dived into darkness. I fell down, down, down, surrounded by the coyote's weird howling. I never reached the bottom, but floated on a wind that blew a gentle cool breath of peanut butter and toothpaste across my face. And the breath whispered in my ear, "I'm waiting, Darien. I'm waiting."

My whole body ached.

Chapter Eight

Every bone in my body was still hurting the next morning.

I tried moving, obviously a mistake because Ringo immediately jumped up on the bed and stuck his cold nose into my face. I pushed him away, groaning. It was all I could do to limp across to the bathroom and back to my bed. My scrapes throbbed almost as much as my ankle. My side was so tender that it hurt to breathe.

Dad stuck his head in my room to say good-bye before he left for work, and Mom brought me up some toast and juice. I must have dozed off again because I woke up with Mom standing beside my bed dressed to go out.

"Will you be okay alone for awhile?" she asked. "I'm going down to the office to check on a few things."

I didn't know what to say, I was so surprised. "Yeah. Sure." I started to grin at her, but my face protested and all she got was a crooked wince. "No problem."

If all it took was for me to rip my body open to put things back together at home, I was a willing sacrifice. And for a while, the cloud around our house did lift. Life was a little easier. Mom and Dad talked to each other again and Mom went back to work a couple of days a week. I missed five whole days of school while my body mended, so I didn't have to deal with any stares. The last two weeks before vacation were mostly field trips and sports days, anyway. Everyone was too busy goofing off to bother with me.

But the cloud settled back over the house long before my scars had time to heal. Mom and Dad talking to each other meant they started to notice me more. What they noticed was that I pretty much came and went as I pleased. Not anymore. They watched everything I did, asked where I was going when I went out and made up crazy rules about not riding my bike on certain roads and not being out after dark. Those were the conditions I had to agree to before they'd get my bike fixed.

They came down hard on not going into the coulees alone. So I either had to start lying or stay in my room the rest of my life. My room had too many memories of Jeri. I became a pretty good liar. I even lied to my friends, coming up with excuses when Brad or Ryan asked me to hang out with them.

It was easier to be alone. I lost myself in the coulees every chance I got. When Ringo and I dropped over the ridge and scrambled down to the bottom, it was like nothing else mattered. Or even existed. Every day I spent down there I felt further and further away from the mess of my life in that other world on top.

Sometimes, in the coulees, I felt the icy

breath of mint on the wind. But even when I didn't, I knew there was something with me. A presence with an emptiness like my own, but also wild and free. It surrounded me as soon as I entered the coulee and stayed with me until I climbed out. It got so I'd wait for it at the same spot every time. And it always came. I felt a rush, a surge of energy like electricity going right through me, and my heart would skip a beat.

A couple of times, lying on a sunny rock watching the sky, I felt someone lying beside me, pointing to shapes in the clouds like I used to do with Jeri. Or running along the river with Ringo, I'd hear Jeri laughing. His presence was so strong I'd sometimes reach out to hold his hand.

Every so often the coyote was there, too. I'd get a sense of despair, almost anger, and look up and see it on the ridge. The uneasiness passed as quickly as the coyote, but I knew the animal was somehow connected to me.

When I was in the coulees, it was almost as if Jeri had never died. I began to hope that if I could only lose myself far enough, one day I would scramble up the slope and he'd be there waiting for me — just like in my dream.

But that wasn't really going to happen. At least, not as long as the coyote was there.

CHAPTER NINE

That's how I spent most days — exploring the coulees with Ringo while Mom and Dad thought I was at Ryan's or Brad's. We stayed away from the rock pile behind the fourth green and found another route to the river.

My favorite place was a couple of coulees upstream, where a chunk of the farmer's field had fallen into the valley. At one place, water running down the slump had caused a cave-in just before the steep riverbank. What was left was a hollow sheltered on both sides by small cliffs. The river swept around a sunny gravel bar into a deep clear pool at the foot of the hollow. It was always quiet and still in there.

One day, a few weeks after school let out, Ringo and I were scrambling up the steep part of the coulee across from our house instead of taking the easy route. I was hanging onto a thick clump of grass, trying to pull myself up over the edge, when I heard a voice.

"It would be a lot easier to climb up somewhere else. Almost anywhere else. There's even a path over there."

I looked up. This skinny kid stood over me, hands in his pockets and a big grin plastered from one ear to the other. In the middle of his grin was a hole the size of my thumb.

"Yeah?" I said. "Maybe I like climbing up here."

"Suit yourself." He scuffed the ground with the toe of his sneaker and turned away.

The clump of grass I was hanging onto began to pull out of the ground. "Hey, you could at least give me a hand," I called.

His grin got even bigger and he reached down. I grabbed his hand and with Ringo barking encouragement, hauled myself up.

"Thanks," I said, brushing the dirt off my jeans and looking him over. His hair was not only straw-colored, it looked like straw. Short, straight blades poking out in all directions. His face made me wonder if someone had taken a whole pail of freckles and dumped it over him. Put him in a pair of overalls and give him a straw to chew on, and you'd think he came straight off the farm. But instead of overalls, he was wearing shorts and a baggy t-shirt with writing across it that said *I get my kicks from soccer*. Who was this kid and what was he doing in my coulee? "You live around here?"

"Just moved here. From Calgary." He pointed across the street at the moving van in the driveway next to our house. "They told me to get lost until the truck is unpacked. My name's Josh. Joshua Michels."

"I live next door. I'm Darien Carey." I tried not to sound too friendly. I just stared at the gap between his front teeth. It was so big, I thought he was missing a tooth. But he wasn't.

"That your dog?"

"Yeah. Ringo."

"I can see why you named him that. Those patches around his eyes are great. He's a cool looking dog."

It was Jeri who'd named him Ringo, but I wasn't about to bring that up with this guy. I didn't say anything and hoped he would go away. Unfortunately, Ringo didn't cooperate. He trotted right over to Josh, wagging his tail in a happy-to-meet-you rhythm. Josh knelt down and scratched Ringo's ears and neck just as if he knew what would make my dog his friend for life. I shot Ringo my best withering glare. Traitor. Josh was oblivious. He kept right on babbling.

"I'm starting grade seven at Stafford Junior High in September. How about you?"

"Yeah, me too. I guess."

"Great! We can ride the bus together. Know anyone else our age who lives around here?"

"Not really," I lied. Lying was almost automatic with me these days.

He shrugged.

I couldn't help myself any longer. "Did you inherit that hole in your face from your mom or your dad?"

He didn't even nibble at the bait.

"Neat, eh?" was all he said. "I can whistle better than anyone I know. Want to hear?" He didn't wait for an answer, but took a huge gulp of air and let out this piercing whistle that sounded like an eagle screaming in my ear. Ringo jumped backwards and yelped. One of the moving men fell off the back of the moving van. He caught the side panel just in time to do a one-handed swing out over the driveway, or he would have ended up on his tailbone. I snickered. I couldn't help myself.

"Where were you hiking?" asked Josh.

The question caught me by surprise and I almost told him about my hollow.

"There's this — Just in the coulee." He waited for more, but I didn't oblige him.

"Any snakes down there?"

"Sure. Lots of rattlers." That would keep him out of my way, I figured. I was wrong.

"Cool. Reptiles are my hobby. Especially

snakes. I have a bull snake at home. Wanna see it?"

"You're kidding. You don't have a pet snake." He was just trying to impress me.

"If you don't believe me, you'll have to come see for yourself."

What could I do? Josh waited while I put Ringo in my back yard. At Josh's house, we dodged the movers hauling a sofa in the door and took the stairs up to his room two at a time.

There on the floor was a glass box like an aquarium, with a snake coiled in the corner. A couple of rocks leaned against each other on the wooden bottom of the box. There was a dish of water beside them.

"I got him for a science project last year and my parents let me keep him."

"How big is he?"

"Only about as long as my bed when he's all stretched out."

As long as his bed seemed awful big to me. "What do you feed him?"

"Mice. But he doesn't eat very often. Once every week or so. He's hardly any work to take care of and he doesn't stink. That's how I convinced my mom to let me keep him."

On top of the cage was a soft kind of screen material. Josh slid it back and reached in slowly, grabbing the snake behind the head. "Want to hold him? His name is Moses. He probably won't bite."

The snake hissed and curved his body in midair. "Probably? Doesn't sound like he wants to be held."

"He's a little nervous maybe, from all the moving. He'll calm down soon. He's usually a pretty easy-going fella."

The memory of rattlesnakes writhing in their nest was too fresh for me to handle any snake. "Uhh. Not now. Some other time," I said.

Josh put Moses back in his cage. Then I realized I had just committed myself to coming back.

"I should be going." I got up from the floor and looked around for the first time. There was a bedframe and mattress leaning against the wall and a pile of boxes stacked in the middle of the floor.

"Yeah. Well, I gotta unpack all this stuff and help Dad set up my furniture," Josh said. "Maybe you could come over again tomorrow."

"Maybe."

Josh showed me out the back door to avoid the movers and I was gone. I didn't plan to return.

CHAPTER TEN

I was back the next morning carrying a pan of lasagna, my mom's idea of a welcome-to-the-neighborhood offering.

"They'll have a big enough job unpacking tomorrow without having to cook," she said when I told her and Dad about our new neighbors. "Darien, you can take the lasagna over in the morning. When they're settled, we'll meet them properly."

So there I was, right where I didn't want to be. I rang the bell and waited, hoping one of Josh's parents would answer and I could just hand over the lasagna and leave. No

such luck. The door opened and there stood
Josh, wearing that huge grin with the hole in
the middle.

"Hi!" He saw the lasagna and yelled over
his shoulder. "Mom! Dad! The delivery
boy's here!"

Mr. Michels stuck his head up over a stack
of boxes and Mrs. Michels walked into the
room, looking confused. "Delivery boy? Did
somebody order a pizza?"

She had the same spiky straw-colored
hair as Josh only she had a kerchief tied
around it so it wasn't sticking out all over.
She was wearing jeans rolled up above her
ankles and a man's shirt at least three sizes
too big for her with the shirt tails tied
around her waist. She wiped her hands on a
towel and wiped the towel across her forehead. It left behind a streak of something
grey.

I couldn't help laughing. "Not pizza.
Lasagna. I'm Darien Carey from next door.
My mom thought you wouldn't have time to
cook today. She thinks take-out is disgusting,
so she sent you this." I held out the pan.

Josh's mom laughed, a nice easy laugh. It reminded me of how long it'd been since *my* mom laughed like that. "I have to agree with her," Mrs. Michels said. "Take-out is disgusting. Thank you, Darien. And please thank your mother." She took the pan from me and disappeared into the kitchen.

"Come on upstairs. I'm almost finished unpacking," said Josh. "Dad, can I go hiking in the coulees with Darien after I'm done?"

His father nodded, though I wasn't so sure he even heard Josh. He was busy hooking up the TV and stereo. "Sure. Nice to meet you, Darien. And thanks for showing Josh around. It's nice to see him making friends so quickly." He looked at the wires in his hand and frowned, then his head disappeared behind the TV.

I couldn't believe my day was planned for me, just like that.

Josh's room was beginning to look like someone lived there. The bed was set up and Moses' glass house sat on a low table in the corner. A dresser had appeared on one wall and a bookcase on another, with a portable

CD player sitting on top.

While Josh finished putting books and trophies into the bookcase, I walked over to say hello to Moses. He didn't move. He looked an awful lot like the rattlesnakes I'd seen in the coulees, kind of a deep yellow-brown color with darker brown splotches along his back and lighter splotches on both sides. A couple of the splotches near his head were stretched out around a big lump.

"What's wrong with your snake?" I said.

"Huh? Oh, nothing's wrong. He just ate, is all. I fed him last night. He's still digesting."

I started to ask what he'd fed him, then thought better of it. I didn't want to know. I leaned on the bookcase and watched Josh.

"I haven't found my CDs yet or we could listen to some music," he said.

I picked up one of the trophies stacked in an open box. It was for soccer. Josh noticed me looking at it. "You play?" he asked.

"Yeah. I used to, anyway. Not this year."

"Why not?"

I shrugged. "Didn't want to."

"I played in Calgary, but I couldn't finish

the season because we moved. Dad got transferred down here."

I nodded as if I knew what it was like to move to a different city even though I'd lived in Lethbridge all my life. I picked up a photo lying on top of Josh's bookcase. It was a family picture, taken outside in some park. Josh looked like he was about eight or nine. His mom and dad looked pretty much the way they did now, and there was an older brother in the photo. I wondered if he was at university or something and that's why I hadn't seen him yet. "How old is your brother?"

It took Josh a minute to answer. "Shane would be nineteen."

Would be?

Then Josh added, "He died in a car accident three years ago."

"Oh." I didn't know what to say. I only knew that saying nothing would be the biggest mistake of all. That's what all my friends said to me about Jeri. Nothing. So I swallowed and stumbled over my words. "Hey. I'm sorry. I thought maybe he was away at university or something."

Josh smiled. "Don't worry. I don't mind people asking about my brother. I like to remember him."

He said it so matter-of-factly. As for me, I tried not to think about Jeri because it hurt so much when I did. Was Josh saying the hurt would go away? If he was, I didn't believe him.

I remembered exactly what it felt like when I first realized my little brother might die. It felt like the biggest fullback on the biggest soccer team in the league had come up behind me and hit me with a tackle that knocked every ounce of breath out of me.

Josh was saying something else, but I barely heard him. The memory film was playing in my head again.

CHAPTER ELEVEN

Jeri's hair fell out a few weeks after he got home from the hospital. All of it. That's when I first got scared. I guess he lost his hair gradually because I didn't really notice until Halloween, Jeri's fifth birthday. Jeri thought Halloween was the best day of the year, of course. He figured he had the same birthday as all the monsters and goblins in the world.

He couldn't have kids over for a party because Mom was worried he might catch something, but we had a family party and we all dressed up in costumes. He wanted to be the Cookie Monster so Mom made him this costume out of long, blue furry stuff. It had a furry blue hat, complete with ears that tied around his chin.

I put blue Halloween make-up on his face to match his costume. When I finished, I sat him on the bathroom counter to pull on his hat. We were looking in the mirror, to get the total effect. That's when I saw just how much hair Jeri had lost. All of it. He saw it, too.

"Look, Dari. I'm bald!" He rubbed his hand back and forth over his hairless head. "See!"

I ran my hand over his smooth scalp. "You're right. No hair."

He didn't seem to mind. In fact, he seemed to forget about it. "Put on the Cookie Monster hat, Dari."

I pulled the blue fur over his head. No more baldness.

"Now I need my cookies. Mom made peanut butter cookies."

Mom also made him a birthday cake shaped like a pumpkin. I thought for a minute it had peanut butter icing, but it was only regular stuff colored orange. There were black licorice bats pouring out of the top of the cake.

During the party, all I could think about was Jeri's bald head. When he'd first come home from the hospital, I couldn't help being a little mad that I'd had to send Ringo away. I guess I was jealous, too. Jeri got so many presents! Mom and Dad bought him stuff to play with at home, Grandma and Grandpa sent gifts, so did my aunts and uncles, and even Jeri's preschool teacher! Books, stuffed animals, tapes, coloring sets, video games. He even got a TV in his room.

He got tons of stuff and no one seemed to know I even existed. But I was kind of proud of Jeri all the same. He was so gutsy! Every week, he let people jab him with needles and put stuff into his body that made him throw up. He came home after his chemotherapy and slept all day he was so tired. He was pale and he lost weight. There were awful dark circles under his eyes and his arms were dotted with needle marks like he was a junkie or something.

None of the gifts made him better and neither did the medicine they gave him, as far as I could see. And now he had no hair. I wanted to get him something, too. I wanted to give him his hair back, but I couldn't.

Early in December, Jeri and I were together in his room. The Christmas specials were on and we were watching *Rudolph the Red-Nosed Reindeer* on TV. Rudolf had just run into the Abominable Snowman. There was a lot of howling and screaming going on, mostly by the Abominable Snowman.

"Turn it off now, Dari." Jeri's voice came out a tired whisper.

"Huh? What'd you say?"

"Turn if off. Okay, Dari?"

"Don't you want to see the end?" I asked.

"No!"

I flipped the TV off with the remote, but I didn't understand. Jeri wasn't scared of monsters. He liked them! "You tired, Jeri?"

"Yeah." He slid further down under the blankets and put his head on my lap. "Was the 'bomble snowman gonna make Rudolph dead?"

"Nah. He wasn't a bad monster, really. Just made lots of noise. Did he scare you?"

Jeri nodded and scrunched up against me. Then he looked around with his eyes wide open. "I gots a secret," he whispered.

"Oh, yeah? Tell me."

"There's a monster lives in the 'ospel." His voice was soft, and a little shaky.

"There's no real monsters, Jeri. They're just make-believe, like the Cookie Monster and the 'bomble snowman." I couldn't pronounce abominable either. His way was better.

"Uh-uh. There's monsters in the 'ospel." He pulled the blankets up under his nose.

I almost laughed, but caught myself. He was really serious. And scared. Usually Jeri talked like a grownup and not a baby.

"There's just doctors and nurses in the hospital. They're not monsters. They're helping you get better."

"Doctor monsters," he whispered. "They're all white. Just like the 'bomble snowman."

I didn't want to argue with him. After

watching what they'd done to Jeri over the last few months, I almost agreed with him.

"You're home now, Jeri. I'm here and Mom and Dad are here. There's no monsters."

He looked unconvinced, but let me tuck him in, just like Mom and Dad did. "You're not scared?" he asked.

"Me? No way. We can't let a few monsters scare us, can we?" I didn't know what to say to him or what to do to make him feel better. Then I got an idea. "I'll be back in a second, Jeri."

I dug through my dresser until I found what I was looking for. My soccer jersey, washed and folded away at the end of last season. It was too small on me anyway.

"Here you go." I held the jersey out to Jeri. "How about you wear some monster armor when you go to the hospital?"

He looked at me suspiciously. "That's your soccer shirt."

"Yeah. But I never got hurt when I wore it, did I? Now you can wear it."

I pulled it on over his bald head and helped him find the sleeves. It fit nice and loose over his pyjamas and hung down below his knees. "Looks good on you. Pretty soon you'll be wearing it to play soccer."

He snuggled down under the blankets. "Thanks, Dari."

"Anytime," I whispered. He was asleep before I shut the light off. I went downstairs where Mom and Dad were reading in the family room. I wanted to know what was going on.

"When's Jeri going to get better?" I demanded.

They looked up from their books. I hadn't noticed the dark bags under Mom's eyes before, almost as bad as the rings under Jeri's eyes. She got up slowly. "Is something wrong?" she asked. "I was just going up to tuck him in for the night."

"He's already asleep," I said. "We were watching TV and he was too scared to watch Rudolf. The 'bomble snowman scared him." I wanted an answer. "When's he going to get better?"

"Come sit down with us, Darien," said Dad.

"You know Jeri's got leukemia," Mom said. "The chemotherapy is helping. His blood counts are getting better."

"But he's not getting better. He's been sick for months and all the stuff the doctors give him just makes him sicker. He's tired and he pukes all the time. And his hair is all gone."

"We know," Mom said. Her voice was so quiet I could hardly hear it.

Dad went over and sat beside her on the sofa. He held her hand and then he turned to me. "The drugs the doctors give him destroy the cancer cells in his blood so the normal cells can grow again. But the poison in the drugs also affects the rest of his body. It's the medicine that makes him throw up and makes his hair fall out. But Darien, that's a small price to pay to have him better again. His hair will grow back."

"So he's going to get better." I still wanted an answer.

"We hope Jeri will be better soon, Darien. But it is possible he may not get well."

"What's that supposed to mean?" I was starting to get mad.

"We have to hope and pray that Jeri's leukemia goes into remission. The drugs have helped, and the doctors are going to start him on radiation treatments too." Dad sighed. "But sometimes when people get leukemia, they die."

My insides cramped themselves into a knot. I stood there, feeling the knot tighten and get harder and harder, colder and colder.

"The doctors are doing everything they can, but cancer is something they don't know a lot about. The treatments they've been giving Jeri haven't worked as well as they hoped." He stopped and looked at Mom. She was crying. "The answer to your question, Darien, is that no one knows."

I didn't want to ask any more questions.

"I'm going to bed." I turned and ran up the stairs, away from the look I saw on their faces. They were the adults, they were supposed to make things right. But that look told me they didn't know any more than I did. And I'd never felt so helpless in all my life.

I lay in bed and felt the knot tighten and freeze until my insides were a lump of ice. The wind blew that night. It rattled the windows and shook the house with a low piercing wail. Only half-asleep, I imagined there were ghosts floating around the house, crying to be let in. That one of the ghosts was Jeri.

Between the shrieks of the wind, I heard the coyotes howl — loud and frantic and close. When they howled like that in winter, Dad said it was because they had made a kill. I was so cold.

I didn't even warm up when, for the first time since he got home, Jeri crept across the hall and crawled into bed with me. He didn't say anything. Just snuggled up close. The coyotes stopped howling after a few minutes, but we both lay there for a long time, shivering.

CHAPTER TWELVE

"Hey. You ready to go?" Josh gave me a strange look. "Is something wrong?"

I must have been staring into space for awhile. Long enough for Josh to finish unpacking his books and stuff. It was the first time my head flipped into memory mode when someone else was around. "Huh? No. I'm fine. Are you done?"

"I can finish the rest later. Let's go."

I still hadn't come up with an excuse to slip away so I shrugged my shoulders and said, "Okay." I was annoyed at having Josh tag along when I'd rather be alone, but it was just for today.

His mom was in the kitchen surrounded by boxes and dishes. It didn't look like we'd have much luck raiding his fridge so we went to my place to throw some food and water bottles into a backpack and collect Ringo. Ten minutes later we were on our way.

We scrambled down the slope of the coulee and stood at the bottom looking at the hills rising above us. I was surprised to feel the familiar presence drift over and around me. I was surprised to still feel it with Josh along.

"It feels weird down here," Josh said.

I turned to look at him. "What do you mean?"

"I don't know. We're only ten minutes from home but it feels like we're so far away from everything. Like we're not even in the city but in some other place." He looked up at the slopes towering above us. "Do you feel like we're not alone?"

Suddenly my private crazy world was no

longer so crazy. Or private. I wasn't the only one who felt something strange down here. But I wasn't about to admit that I hung out in the coulees with my brother's ghost. Oh, man! This was too much.

I shook my head. "You're nuts. Let's go." Just forget about it, I thought.

We followed my regular trail and, halfway down, came across the deer carcass. It was dried up and rotted. There was no meat left, only bones and bits of skin. I didn't want to show him my hollow by the river so I led him over the ridge beside the fourth green.

"You like snakes, right?" I said.

"Yeah. Why?"

I pointed to the rocks below us. "There was a whole den of rattlers down there earlier this summer. I almost stepped on them."

"No kidding? Are they still there?"

I took a step onto the rocks. There was no warning signal, no cold breath of air. Just a couple of marmots sunning themselves. They scuttled away under the rocks. "I don't think so. Let's check it out."

"Darien, maybe we shouldn't . . ." Josh's voice was a little wary, but I was confident that the snakes weren't there.

"Throw me a stick or something," I said.

Using the stick to probe ahead of me, I scrambled down to the flat rock. Josh followed. Nothing moved. I saw something in a crack between the rocks. I poked the stick into the crack and snagged a perfectly intact snakeskin, withered and shrivelled. You could see each individual scale.

I shuddered a little, but Josh said, "Awesome!"

We put the skin carefully in the front pocket of my pack so it wouldn't get crushed and kept moving towards the river.

This time of year, the water was shallow along shore, but there was a deeper channel in the middle that sped around the bend in little rapids.

We stripped off our t-shirts and tossed them on the stony riverbank with our shoes and other stuff, wading into the river in our shorts. We floated on our backs in the current, Ringo swimming along beside us. A flock of white pelicans glided high above, almost like they were caught in the same current. After the river swept us around the bend, we waded back upstream and did it again. When we got tired of swimming we played our own version of fetch with Ringo. We tossed a stone the size of a softball into the shallow water and Ringo would go down after it, bring it back and drop it at our feet. Except it was never the same stone that we tossed in and we both broke out laughing each time he brought back the wrong one.

We finally got bored laughing at Ringo and just sat on the shore in the sunshine. Josh whistled at the hawks on the cliff across the river until they got tired of screaming back at him and took off.

Josh noticed the scars still healing on my back and asked me about them. I told him how I tried to ride my bike down the coulee, and pointed to the slope.

"You rode your bike down there?" he said, his eyes wide.

"Yeah."

"Are you crazy?"

I laughed. "Maybe."

We ate lunch beside the river. It was one of those summer days when the sky is blue and huge and empty and seems real close to the ground. I felt like I could reach up and touch it. No clouds, not even a wisp. Just blue, blue sky smelling of sunshine and resting on top of us like a warm blanket.

Neither of us felt like going home, so we walked back through the woods. The trees were small along the river, but further back towards the golf course there were some fair-sized cottonwoods, all bent over with age. "Hey, you like climbing trees?" I asked Josh.

"Sure."

"There's a couple of good ones over here." I threw the pack down and we picked a big tree with a sloping trunk that was easy to climb. We came to a place where the trunk split into two. The branches were low enough for us to grab onto and pull ourselves up. We had a pretty good view of the golf course from there, and could see a group on the fifth tee box. Their drives landed right in front of us on the fairway.

"There's a nest up there," I said, pointing. "I'm gonna take a look." I knew there wouldn't be any eggs in it this late in the year. It was just a challenge to see if I could reach it.

"It's pretty high, Darien. Be careful."

I ignored Josh and pulled myself up a little higher. It was further up than I'd thought, but I'd already dared myself so I couldn't go back now. I grabbed hold of a branch above my head for balance and placed my foot on the next fork.

I could feel the branch shift under my weight. The whole top of the tree seemed to sway. Now I was just below the nest. I looked around for another hold higher up and began to reach for it.

That's when things went wrong. Something whizzed past my head and hit the tree with a thunk! I was so startled I let go of the branch and jerked away. My foot slipped and I fell backwards, bouncing around in the branches like the golf ball that had just missed me. Except I was bigger and fell harder.

Branches broke under me, jabbed me, scratched me on the way down. I tried to grab one, but I was moving too fast. I closed my eyes and felt a current of cold air flow under me.

The ground came up and met my back with a solid thud. But I felt like I was landing in water. I gasped for breath and let my heart drop back into place. A cold breeze drifted along my body and over my face, just long enough for me to catch a whiff of peanut butter. Then it was gone. Ringo was beside me, whining and turning around in circles.

Josh scrambled down the tree and jumped from the last branch to the ground beside me. "Are you okay?"

"Yeah," I gasped. "I think so." I stayed where I was for another minute and then propped myself up on my elbows. I grabbed Ringo and held him, scratching under his collar.

"Geez, you scared me!"

"I scared me, too."

I stood up and felt around. My legs were

like rubber but nothing seemed broken. Just a few scratches and welts from the branches that broke my fall. Was it only the branches? I remembered the cold air that buoyed me up on the way down and touched my face after I landed.

Josh looked at me and shook his head. "I think you are crazy. Why'd you climb so high?"

"It didn't look so high at first. I would have made it except for somebody's lousy drive."

There was the golf ball lying under the tree. Which meant the golfers would be coming after it. I turned and looked and sure enough, they were walking down the fair-way towards us. "Let's get out of here."

I grabbed the golf ball as compensation for my injuries, and threw the backpack over my shoulder. We took off through the trees, running until we were back on the coulee trail home, Ringo chasing at our heels all the way. Then we stopped long enough to check the damage more closely. Not too bad, considering. A scraped knee and some scratches. I'd wear long pants until the scrapes healed and no one would even know. Except Josh. "Hey, don't say anything to my parents, okay? They're always on my case and if they find out, the next thing they'll do is not let me go hiking anymore."

He didn't say anything for a bit and then nodded. "Yeah. Sure. But next time you try killing yourself, wait till I'm not around."

"I wasn't . . ." Ahh, forget it. I didn't care what he thought. I hadn't wanted him around in the first place. I muttered under my breath, "I never asked you to tag along, did I?"

He didn't answer. We started back together and by the time we climbed up to our street, he seemed to have forgotten all about being ticked off. We stopped in front of my house, but I didn't invite him in. I took the snakeskin out of my pack and gave it to him.

"Your knee okay?" he asked.

"Just a scratch. I'll wash it and no one will even notice."

"See you t'morrow?"

"I gotta do some stuff with my mom tomorrow." I lied before I even thought about it and suddenly I realized I'd had a pretty good time with Josh.

He looked a little hurt for a second, but then he shrugged. "Okay. Catch you later then."

Ringo barked a friendly farewell. "Yeah, later." I went inside and started to rinse off my knee.

CHAPTER THIRTEEN

I woke up late the next morning from a sleep without nightmares.

Mom was at work so I had the house to myself. She'd left a note on the kitchen table to say she'd be home for lunch. I thought about going for a walk in the coulees but I didn't want Josh to see me after I'd told him I was busy. So I stayed in and watched music videos on TV. It didn't take long before I'd had enough of that, so I picked up a book. But I didn't really feel like reading either. Ringo sat by the front door whining to go out.

"Be quiet, Ringo," I snapped. I threw the TV Guide at him. He gave me a disgusted look and trotted upstairs.

I finally admitted that I was bored and lonely. I almost wanted to call Josh or one of my other friends. I remembered the photo of Josh's family and what he said about his brother. I wandered upstairs to Jeri's room.

Ringo poked his head around the corner and stood there, watching me climb the stairs. Then he trotted calmly across the hall, his claws clacking on the hardwood floor, and walked into Jeri's room ahead of me. When I stopped at the doorway, he turned and gave a little bark as if he was inviting me in.

For the first time since Jeri died, I stepped into his room.

The instant I entered, I was surrounded by the same feeling I got in the coulees. Someone was here, with me. Someone full of calm and light.

The room looked just like always. Jeri's bed neatly covered with his Sesame Street quilt. His stuffed Big Bird, Cookie Monster, and Bert and Ernie sitting together against the pillows. The dresser beside the bed with a few of his favorite toys on top.

The window was open slightly and the curtains drifted in and out on the breeze. Mom must have decided to air out the room. I sat on Jeri's bed and the memories started to float in with the breeze from the window.

This time, I remembered the Sunday morning in February when I woke up early and went to Jeri's room to see how he was doing. He was sleeping, so I stood there for awhile, looking out his window at the backyard and the coulee behind it. There were some mule deer on the slope behind our fence.

"Is it morning?"

I turned at the sound of Jeri's voice. He was sitting up in bed, wearing the soccer jersey I gave him.

"Yeah. But it's early. Mom and Dad are still sleeping." I waved at him to come over to the window. "Put on your slippers and come here."

He slid off the bed and scrunched his feet

into his slippers, the ones with Bert on one foot and Ernie on the other. "What is it?"

"Come look at the deer."

I lifted him up so he was standing on the sill and leaning against me. Just then, five or six deer leaped over the fence into our yard. They walked across the skiff of snow on the lawn like they owned the place and started nibbling on the cedars Dad had planted in the back yard.

"They're havin' breakfast," Jeri whispered.

"Yeah, on Dad's bushes." We both laughed, quietly. "There's a little one, see, Dari?" He pointed to a small deer that was sticking close to its mom.

We watched them for a long time until a neighbor's door slammed. The deer lifted their heads in unison at the sound. They trotted back to the fence, leaped over and were gone.

"How come they left?" Jeri wanted to know.

"They heard the noise and got scared."

"We wouldn't hurt 'em."

"No. But they don't know that. They have to be careful."

"Maybe they think it was coyotes."

"Maybe."

"If I was outside, I'd be scared of coyotes."

I lifted him up and set him back on his bed. Once I would have tossed him there. "You don't need to be scared, Jeri. If you get scared when the coyotes howl or the wind blows, you just come and stay with me in my room, okay?"

"Okay." He pointed his finger at me. "And if you get scared, you come to my room and stay with me."

"Deal," I said, trying not to let him see in my eyes how scared I was.

The memory faded and Jeri's room came back into focus slowly. I blinked my eyes. For once my insides weren't hard or icy. They were empty, hollow. I felt like my chest might collapse. I used to think all those songs about someone's heart aching were just words, but a person's heart really can ache so that there's a big pain inside. The ache came over and over again in waves that

made my heart pound until I thought it
would burst.

I wanted to scream. I opened my mouth to
scream.

And then the light in the room suddenly
got brighter and started to come together
and move into a cool stream of air that was
familiar to me. The air with the light inside
it swirled and wrapped itself around me. As
it whispered past my face, I smelled minty
coolness and peanut butter all mixed up
together. The scent floated by me, so that I
turned my head to follow it.

Inside me, the waves stopped crashing
against my heart, the swells of hurt dis-
solved. Then the light stopped shining, and
the room was still. I felt battered and tired,
but also calm and peaceful.

"Oh, Jeri. I miss you," I whispered.

I closed my eyes and tried not to move,
wanting to hang on to the sense of peace.

I must have fallen asleep, because when I
opened my eys, the light in the room was
flat. The sun was behind some clouds. The

wind had picked up and the breeze coming in the window was cold.

I walked over and closed the window. When I turned around again, I thought I saw a shimmer over Jeri's bed. For just a second there was a quiver in the air where I'd been lying. Then it was gone.

Ringo still sat at the door, whining quietly.

I straightened the quilt, smoothed the wrinkles from Big Bird, and picked up the Cookie Monster that had fallen on the floor. When I reached over to put him back in his place, I noticed the corner of something sticking out from under the pillow. I lifted the pillow and saw my soccer jersey, folded neatly. I held it to my face and breathed in. It smelled ever so faintly of Jeri. I smiled and put it back where I found it.

"Come on, Ringo. Let's go."

I left the door open.

CHAPTER FOURTEEN

I wasn't scared that I was going crazy anymore. Because I knew now that Jeri was with me. And if that meant I was crazy, that was fine with me.

Part of me had known it since the time by the river when something pushed me away from the snakes, but I couldn't admit it to myself until now. Jeri couldn't be here in person so he was here in spirit. My own private ghost. Or angel.

There was no other explanation. I remembered hearing somewhere that when all possible explanations don't work, try the impossible.

So when Mom told me she was going to pack up Jeri's room and give his stuff to the Salvation Army, I threw my first tantrum since I was four.

"No!"

"What on earth has got into you, Darien?"

"Just leave his room alone!"

Dad heard the commotion and started up the stairs. "What's going on up here?"

I yelled at Dad. "Mom's going to give all Jeri's stuff away!"

"Oh, honey." Mom sighed and sat on Jeri's bed. "I'm not going to give all his things away. We'll go through his room together and keep some special things to remember him by. But it's time to let him go, Darien. He's not coming back to his room and he doesn't need his clothes anymore."

I could see how hard it was for her to say that. Her face was pale, she was trembling and her voice shook. Dad went over and put his arm around her. But I still wanted to scream at them. I wanted to scream, "He's come back and he needs his room to stay like it is or he'll go away again!" I couldn't say that though, so I said the only other thing I could think of.

"No! If you pack up his room, we'll stop remembering him. I won't let you!"

Mom started to cry softly.

"Darien, we won't do anything that upsets you so much," Dad said finally. "And you know we'll never forget Jeri. But we have to accept the fact that he's not coming back. We have to start trying to be a family again."

I didn't say anything. They weren't going to take Jeri's room apart. That's all I cared about. I stood in the doorway with my arms crossed and glared.

Dad could see he wasn't going to get anywhere with me on the subject. "We'll talk later when everyone has calmed down."

There wasn't anything they could say to me later that was going to change how I felt. The only reason I let them pack up Jeri's clothes was because they promised they'd leave the rest of his room the way it was.

That's when they brought up the subject of going to talk to a shrink, only they called it a counselor. I got up and walked away. If everyone would just leave me alone, I'd be fine.

Mom and Dad did back off then. The one I couldn't get to back off was Josh.

The next day, he showed up at the front door with a backpack full of sandwiches and before I could come up with an excuse, Dad hustled me out the door.

The rest of the summer seemed to follow the same pattern. Once in a while, Ringo and I managed to sneak off on our own, but even when we did, Josh usually found us. I tolerated him because Jeri, or Jeri's ghost, seemed to tolerate him. At least the familiar feeling didn't disappear when Josh was there.

Jeri's ghost is what got me through the summer. During the day Jeri was alive again, running with Josh and me in the coulees, splashing in the river and sunning on the rocks.

But my nightmares got worse. The black shape of the coyote no longer just howled at me and Jeri. It stalked us, slinking through the prairie grasses, the coulees, the woods. I woke, always at the same instant, when the dark shape started to materialize into cold eyes and bared fangs, reaching for Jeri while I stood and watched. And then one night at the end of summer, I was getting ready for bed and happened to glance out my window. My eyes were pulled out over the prairie to a shadow that seemed to move. I walked to the window to get a better look.

The wind was working its way up to a full-force gale and the trees bowed down away from it. An old tumbleweed blew across the yard below me. The moon was almost full, shining bright in the night sky, and the lawn looked like a sea of cold silver light and deep shadows.

Then I saw it. On the edge of the prairie just before the light gave way to blackness, a dark shape sat motionless, watching me. It lifted its head and opened its mouth and then I knew it wasn't only the wind howling into my room.

I couldn't move. I just stood there, looking

at the coyote. It had found me. My nightmare had become real.

I crawled into bed and lay there, scared and shivering, for a long time. It wasn't until a familiar touch drifted across my face that I finally fell asleep, too tired to dream.

CHAPTER FIFTEEN

School started right after Labor Day. Josh was at my front door to pick me up that first morning, just like I knew he would be. We rode the bus together.

Grade seven — junior high — was going to be a different story than last year. We were the peons now. The kids in grade eight and nine looked at us like we were scum, unfit to breathe the same air they did. The only good thing was most of them didn't know anything about Jeri so I didn't feel like an alien. Josh was getting the same treatment I was, and so were Brad, Ryan, Eric and Tyler and all the rest of the "infants". That was one of the nicer terms I heard aimed in our direction.

I introduced Josh to the others on the bus and in no time he was busy telling them about Moses and coulee climbing all summer. I tuned out after awhile and stared out the bus window. Brad turned around in his seat and looked at me.

"You doing okay now?" he asked.

I almost ignored him, out of habit more than anything, but when I looked at his face I saw he was really worried. Suddenly I felt bad about brushing him off so many times. So I shrugged back at him. "I guess. Better anyway."

He grinned. "Good." And then his smile disappeared. "I'm sorry, Darien. About your brother." He looked down at the floor of the bus, which hadn't had time to collect more than a bit of dirt from our sneakers. "And I'm sorry I didn't tell you that last spring."

It was the last thing I expected to hear. At first I wasn't sure what to say. It wasn't like those few words made everything okay or made things like they used to be. But maybe my friends *did* care, even if they didn't know what to do or say. I looked back at Brad and managed a smile. "Thanks."

I could see Josh looking at us and wondering what we were talking about, but he didn't say anything.

"Soccer playoffs start next week," Brad continued in a hurry. "We could use a team manager for the playoffs. Someone to look after water bottles, equipment. Stuff like that."

I smirked at him. "You think I'm gonna fetch your water for you?"

He grinned. "Just until you start playing again next season. We really need another goal scorer. Some days we couldn't put the ball in the ocean."

"You never could," I said with a straight face.

He took off his ball cap and aimed a swat at my head. I ducked.

I ignored the muttered insults of the older kids and the first week back went pretty good. Most of my teachers seemed okay and it was a relief not to have everyone watching me like I was going to fall apart. Then on Friday, I had phys. ed. after lunch. It was the last class of the day because we got out early on Fridays. Mr. McLean started us off with a soccer unit, and after doing a bunch of dribbling and passing drills, we scrimmaged. I played defence, not my favorite position, not to mention the fact that I hadn't played all summer.

Soon after the scrimmage started I messed up a pass to one of our halfbacks. The other team intercepted the ball and in one quick run downfield, they scored.

"Nice going, Carey," said one of the guys on my team, Scott Peterson. He walked over to me. "Thought you were some hotshot soccer player."

I ignored him, but Brad wasn't so ready to let it go. "Leave him alone, Scott," he shot back.

Scott's reply came out of nowhere. "What's the matter? We're supposed to feel sorry for him because he lost his baby brother? It's old news."

I stopped dead, the breath knocked right out of me. My body went cold and hollow. All the noises on the field faded behind a ringing in my ears. Suddenly I was tired of holding it all in, tired of walking away from people and just tired of everything.

I could feel the knot in my stomach uncoil and snap as my fist smashed into Scott's face. I felt my knuckles crunch against his nose and saw the astonishment in his eyes. Then I turned and walked off the field. Mr. McLean yelled over at me, but I ignored him.

I grabbed my clothes from the locker room, stuffed everything into my pack and headed right out of school. It was too early for the school bus so I walked a block over and hopped on a city bus.

I got off on our street and kept going, not thinking, over the prairie and down the coulee to my private hollow overlooking the river. The knot in my stomach was coiled tight again.

It's old news. Old news. Those words kept going around in my head. But Jeri's death wasn't old news. It felt like it just happened yesterday and nothing had been real ever since. Not the fact that he was dead, not the crazy things I'd been seeing and smelling, not the nightmares and not even the routine things like eating a meal with my parents or riding the bus to school.

The September sun was hot and the hollow was an oven where the rocks gathered the heat and held it. I sat on the edge of a jutting rock ledge and stared at the water moving quietly below me. Along the river valley, the coulees folded one on top of the other all the way to the horizon where they turned into mountain peaks rising into the sky. An early snow high up in the mountains dusted their tops and made them glisten in the sunshine.

I waited for the feeling of safety and power that usually surrounded me in the coulees, the one place I still felt any control. It didn't come. There was only a stillness. Not even a bird called. I kept waiting, moving further away in my mind with every minute that passed.

The footsteps were close before I heard

them. Josh came up behind me and sat down on the rock. He looked out over the river flowing past us and the clear pool below, at the cliffs wrapping themselves around us on three sides.

"Nice spot," he said finally.

I threw a pebble into the water and watched it drift to the bottom.

"So this is where you go when you ditch me." His words threw me off balance. I stared at him. "You really think I don't know when I'm being ditched?"

I threw another stone into the water. He tossed one in after mine. "So why didn't you ever say anything?" I asked him.

"I thought you maybe had something to figure out, you know. By yourself."

"Yeah."

"I didn't know about your brother. Brad told me after you decked Scott and took off. Scott was so surprised he didn't even say anything when Brad told Mr. McLean that Scott had caught an elbow in the face on the last play. McLean didn't see what really happened."

"Scott's a jerk."

"Definitely." He tossed another rock in the pool. "Nice of Brad to cover up for you, though. I think he's missed you. Sounds like you used to hang out a lot."

I nodded. "I suppose we did. Played soccer and stuff."

"So what happened?" I could see Josh was going to keep pushing. But for once I didn't mind.

"I just didn't feel like playing after Jeri died."

He nodded. "I remember when Shane died. I was so mad at him. I still am sometimes."

Again he surprised me. "Mad at Shane?"

"Yeah, you know, for dying. For not being more careful driving and for dying and leaving me alone."

I thought about that. "I'm not mad at Jeri. I'm mad at the doctors who were supposed to help him and couldn't do anything. I'm mad at Mom and Dad, because they're not supposed to let things like this happen. I'm mad that no one could do anything. Including me."

I added quietly, barely able to force the words out, "Jeri didn't deserve to die." Saying it like that, the knot in my stomach loosened a bit.

"I don't know that anyone really deserves to die," Josh said. "That's just the way it is. People are born and people die. We can't live without dying."

"So why do some people like Jeri and Shane have to die before they get a chance to live?" My voice cracked. I threw a rock far out into the river.

"I don't know. I don't know why Shane had to die before he got to teach me how to drive or take me to a Jays' game like he always promised. But I know I can't change what happened. And I'm really glad he was my brother even if I don't get to have him around anymore."

I thought of Jeri tackling me in the yard and making "samwitches" and sneaking in to sleep with me at night. "You could have told me about Jeri, you know," Josh said. "It's a whole lot easier to take if you tell somebody."

I did feel better. But talking about it still hurt like hell. "How'd you find me?"

"It wasn't hard. I figured you'd be in the coulees somewhere and you've just about got a path worn to this place. It is kinda different down here, isn't it? Peaceful."

I closed my eyes and realized the familiar presence was still there, faint, but calm and cool around me. I took a deep breath, scared to say what I wanted to tell him next. "When I'm in the coulees, you know, I can feel Jeri here with me. Like none of it ever happened and he's smiling and happy just like always."

"Yeah. I can see that. This place does that for you."

"You don't think I'm crazy?" I held my breath.

"Why would I think that?"

"Josh, I really feel him, you know. I even smell him sometimes. It's like he's right there."

Chapter Fifteen

"What do you mean? Like he's a ghost?"

"I don't know. It's not scary like a ghost would be. It's more like he's just keeping me company, hanging out."

"I like to think that when Shane died, a part of him stayed with me."

"Like a ghost, a spirit of some kind?"

He nodded, slowly. "Maybe when people die, God lets them come back to see how we're doing."

Neither of us said anything for a long time. Then Josh added, "I think the people who love us still love us even if they die."

I shook my head. "I think we're both nuts. Ghosts, angels, phantom coyotes. None of it's real."

Josh's head snapped up. "Phantom coyotes?"

"Forget it," I said, standing up. "You hear the coyotes howling at night sometimes, don't you?"

"Sure. They howl all the time."

"I just dream about a coyote once in awhile, that's all. And a couple of times I've seen one at night when I looked out my window."

135

"Where?"

"On top of the coulee ridge across from our house. It sits there and watches me. It feels . . ." I struggled to find the right word. ". . . wrong. Angry."

I waited for Josh to laugh. But he was quiet. After awhile he said, "Have you told anyone?"

"Why should I tell anyone? It's just a coyote."

"Then why do you think it watches you?"

"I just do. I can feel it."

"Well, at night sometimes, things feel one way when they really aren't."

"I know. But this isn't like that."

He stood up beside me and brushed the dust off his jeans. "So what are we going to do about it?"

"I don't know what we're going to do about it." I looked at him, not smiling one bit. "But I'm tired of letting it scare me."

Chapter Sixteen

After that, I stopped making excuses when I didn't want Josh around. If I wanted to be alone, I just told him and he would call me later. But more and more, I wanted to hang out with him. A couple of times Brad and Ryan joined us and we spent the warm September afternoons in the coulees after school, Ringo running along beside us. Sometimes we went over to Josh's place and let Moses crawl over our laps and around our arms and shoulders. Or Josh and Ringo and I went to the soccer games and watched Brad and Ryan play.

One day at noon, when Josh and I were walking back to school from the Mac's store, we saw a bunch of cars pull up at a church nearby. There was a black hearse and a limo parked in front of the church. I stopped and watched the people going in.

Jeri's funeral was the only one I'd ever been to, and then I only went to the church, not to the cemetery for the burial. The church had been full. But I hadn't really seen the people, only felt their eyes on me like a thousand clinging spiderwebs. I walked between Mom and Dad up the aisle, and all I saw was the white coffin at the front. Jeri was in there. Jeri was in there. All through the service, that's all I could think about. I didn't hear the music or what the minister said. I didn't cry. My eyes never left the coffin. Jeri was in there.

After the service, Mom and Dad got in a black car behind the hearse and I went home with my aunt and uncle and cousins. Mom and Dad said it was my choice, and I chose not to go to the cemetery. I didn't want to see Jeri put into the ground. I went home and while they buried Jeri, I was laughing.

The adults had gone inside to get food ready for the people who would be coming over later. Me and my three cousins, Gary, Jason and Amy, went out to the back yard.

It was one of the first warm days that spring, and we kicked a soccer ball around in the grass. Soon we had a game of two on two going, me and Amy against Gary and Jason. We were getting blown away, because Amy was only eight and wasn't making much of a contribution. She got mad, too, every time Gary or Jason stole the ball from her.

"Quit that!" she yelled.

"You gotta be faster, Amy!" Gary laughed. Then he dribbled past her and scored again.

I got the ball and brought it back, dribbled up the lawn and passed it to Amy. Gary came at her again. This time, she took a run at him and, with both arms straight out, pushed him right over the ball. Then she calmly kicked the ball back to me and I scored. All three of us broke out laughing at Gary.

"You gotta be faster, Gary!" I mimicked.

He scowled at me and growled at Amy. "You can't push people in soccer, stupid!"

"Can, too. No ref."

"Okay," he said, and launched himself at her. Soon they were rolling in the grass in their good clothes, screaming and giggling. I watched them, laughing. And then I remembered rolling in the grass with Jeri, and that he wasn't here anymore. I stopped laughing, dropped the ball and walked into the house.

Now, the black cars Josh and I saw at the church near our school were lined up behind the hearse, just like they'd been at Jeri's funeral.

"Let's stay," I said to Josh. "I want to see if they go to the cemetery."

He stopped and looked at me. "What do you mean?"

"I want to go to the cemetery and watch them bury the guy."

Josh didn't take to the idea. He gave me a strange look. "What are you on?"

"Come on, Josh. It won't hurt anybody."

"You're so weird," he said. "Why would

you want to see someone you don't even know get buried?"

"I just do." Then I asked him. "Did you go to your brother's funeral?"

"Yeah, of course."

"Did you go to the cemetery after, too?"

He just nodded. "It was awful."

"I never went. To the cemetery, I mean." He looked at me. I didn't blink. "Come on. No one will see us."

"What if they do?"

"They won't. I'm going with or without you."

He shook his head, but still came along. We hung out in the alley behind the church until the doors opened. Six guys wheeled the coffin out. They lifted it down the stairs and into the hearse. People began walking to their cars and then the hearse and limos pulled away.

I turned to Josh. "Come on!" I said.

Josh and I cut through a couple of alleys and streets to get ahead of the cars. It wasn't far to the cemetery. We ran through the gates and crouched inside a clump of thick bushes close to the only open grave. Just then the cars turned the last corner before the entrance. We watched as they parked in a long line. Then the coffin was carried over to the grave, and put on straps that stretched across the hole in the ground. The priest said a few words, but we couldn't hear them. People cried. The wind picked up so that the men's jackets made flapping noises and women hung onto their hats. When the priest finished, they lowered the coffin into the grave and threw a couple of shovelfuls of dirt on it.

After everyone left, Josh and I crept out of the bushes and looked around. The place was deserted. We snuck up to the edge of the grave and looked down. They had only lowered the coffin part way. It was all shiny and new, so smooth that almost all the dirt they tossed in slid right off. A few wilting flowers lay on top.

"Why didn't they put the coffin all the way the grave?" I asked.

"I think they wait until everyone's left

and then someone comes to finish burying it," Josh said.

"Is this the way they did it when your brother died?"

He nodded and looked up at me. "Is he here?"

I knew what he meant. "I think so," I said.

"Where?"

We looked and looked, wandering between the rows of graves. Finally in a new section, we found it. The light brownish-pink headstone had words carved into the stone. They said, *Jeremiah Carey, Oct. 31, 1989 – April 2, 1995. To bless such souls as these, the Lord of Angels came.*

Grass grew over a low mound in front of the headstone and flowers bloomed at the foot of the grave. The grass and the flowers were bending over in the wind. We stayed there a long time.

Finally I looked up at Josh standing beside me. "Let's go," I said.

We ran with the wind back to school. We got there just before the last bell rang and jumped on the bus for home with everyone else.

Lying in bed that night, I looked across the hall through the open door into Jeri's room. He wasn't coming back. His ghost was keeping him here with me in a way, but he really wasn't coming back.

I crept to the window. Even before I looked out, I knew the coyote was there. The wind carried its howl through the night to my room, twisting it into blended shades of fury and loss. It was such a lonely sound.

When I went to sleep, the sound carried me back into my nightmare, where it was dark and almost winter and the black shadow of the coyote stood growling between me and Jeri. I had the same dream every night from then on until Halloween.

On the night before Halloween, I had a different dream.

CHAPTER SEVENTEEN

Something was wrong. I felt a cold sticky dampness against my chest. I looked down at Jeri. The last thing I remembered was reading to him. The book was still on my lap. We must have fallen asleep.

Then I saw the blood. Jeri's blood. His nose was bleeding. It bled all over the front of his pyjamas and my pyjamas and the sheets. Everywhere I looked there was blood. I swallowed and let out the breath I was holding. I didn't want to scare Jeri, but I had to do something.

"Jeri, wake up." I shook him and at the same

time called, "Mom! Dad!" I tried to keep the panic out of my voice.

Mom took one look at the blood covering both of us and swept Jeri into her arms. He was awake now and crying. "It's okay, honey." Mom held him against her. "Just another nose bleed. We'll go see the doctor, okay, and he'll make it stop."

And then they were out the door. Dad stayed long enough to say, "Do your best to clean up in here, okay, Darien? I'll come back as soon as I can."

They were gone and I was sitting in blood. Jeri's blood. Jeri's no-good blood. I picked up my pillow and threw it across the room. It left a dark red smudge on the wall.

Then I ripped off my pyjamas and threw them, together with Jeri's sheets, into the sink in the laundry room. I filled the sink with water and left everything there.

By the time Dad came back to get me, I was dressed and sitting at the kitchen table.

"How is he?" I held my breath.

"They stopped the bleeding and he's getting a blood transfusion now. Do you want to go see him or are you too tired? It's late."

"He's okay?"

"He's okay, Darien."

I started to cry then, and couldn't stop. Dad came over and put his arms around me and held me like I was five again. He cried, too. When I finally lifted my head and pulled away from him, he looked at me through red swollen eyes and smiled.

"Well, we needed that I guess." He picked up the box of tissues, took one and handed the box to me. We both blew our noses. "Ready to go?"

I nodded.

Jeri looked like a ghost lying in the clean white sheets of the hospital bed. He had a tube hooked up to him that was slowly draining a plastic bag of blood into his veins. He smiled at me, but he was half-asleep and drifted off almost right away. Soon, Dad and me went home again. But Mom decided to stay the night with Jeri.

His blood tests showed the leukemia was back. Jeri had to stay in the hospital again. That meant more chemotherapy and more radiation treatments.

Every day after school, I told my friends I was

busy and went to visit him. I read him stories or watched TV with him. Some days, I just watched him sleep. At night, I did my homework while Mom and Dad stayed at the hospital.

One day early in April, Mr. Stevens came to the classroom to get me. Dad was waiting in the office and we walked out together to the car.

"Jeri died this morning," was all he said.

I sat there in the car, watching the world dissolve in front of me.

My stomach was ice.

Chapter Eighteen

When I woke up Halloween morning, I was crying. I wiped the tears from my eyes and sat up.

It was Jeri's sixth birthday.

The wind was blowing hard. It was a cold wind, with lots of winter in it, that whipped the last of the dead leaves off the bare tree limbs and scattered them across our lawn and street. Only skeletons remained, lined up in front of the houses, tall and ready.

For a minute, I forgot everything that'd happened and only remembered that it was

Halloween and Jeri's birthday. I imagined the party we would have for him and wondered whether he would still fit into his Cookie Monster costume. I planned how I would take him trick-or-treating with me and my friends that night. I imagined it so hard, I thought it was real.

Outside, the wind howled louder. It shook the window panes and threw dirt and pebbles from the back alley against the glass. It howled so loud I almost went to the window to see if the coyote was back. Instead, I looked across the hall to Jeri's room. It was empty. Of course.

Jeri died last April. He got a blood clot from the radiation treatments and it caused a stroke and he died in his sleep. There wasn't going to be any birthday party today and he wasn't ever going to turn six or seven or any other age. He'd never be trick-or-treating with me and my friends again.

Angry at the trick my mind played on me, I pulled on jeans and a sweatshirt and got ready for school. I was shaking, not only because I was mad, but because I was scared

— scared that maybe I could no longer tell what was real and what wasn't.

Mom didn't come down for breakfast that morning. Dad was at the counter making toast when I went in the kitchen.

"Want some?" he said.

"Sure."

He put two pieces of toast in front of me. I reached for the peanut butter and then changed my mind and ate the toast plain.

"It's really blowing today." Dad sat down with me at the table.

I nodded and kept munching.

"What are your plans for tonight?"

"Me and the guys are going trick-or-treating right after dinner. Can we eat early?"

"Isn't there a party at school you could go to instead? I'm not sure I like the idea of trick-or-treating these days."

"Dad, we'll be fine. There's a whole group of us and we won't do anything dumb. And we'll just be in our neighborhood. Halloween wouldn't be Halloween without trick-or-treating."

He didn't say anything, just held his cup

of coffee in front of his face without drinking. When he did talk, his voice was so quiet I could hardly hear.

"Okay, Darien. Just promise me you'll be careful."

"Sure, Dad."

After school, I made a sandwich for myself before Dad even got home from work. Mom was still in her bedroom with the door closed. I didn't want to disturb her so I snuck around the kitchen quietly.

But when I went to put on my werewolf mask, Ringo started to bark. No wonder. The mask was more like a whole werewolf head, really. Rough, wild hair grew thick around glowing eyes, and a gaping mouth with long bared fangs dripped bloody ooze. It was so real it gave me the creeps even in daylight. You could practically smell the bad breath.

The rest of the costume was this thick hairy bodysuit with torn shreds of clothing hanging off it. It was the best. As soon as I saw it, I wanted it. Even though it terrified me. I think I had to prove to myself I wasn't scared of it — or of the coyote the costume reminded me of. I begged long and hard before Mom and Dad bought it for me. They finally gave in, probably because it was the first time I was enthusiastic about anything since Jeri died.

But Ringo sure didn't like it. I took off the head. "Quiet!" I hissed at him.

He stopped barking, but he still bounded in circles around me, whining and sniffing.

"It's okay. It's just me, you dumb dog. If you don't shut up, I'll leave you at home." He stopped finally, but I didn't put the head back on until Josh rang the doorbell and we left to meet the others.

I forgot all about my promise to Dad before I even walked out the door.

CHAPTER NINETEEN

The wind was blowing harder than ever.

It wailed in our ears as we ran from house to house yelling, "Trick or treat," jumping out at each other from behind bushes and laughing at the dirty looks from parents walking with their little kids. Only a couple of years ago, we were those little kids, hanging on to Mom and Dad in the dark. But today we were the black shadows we once cringed from, moving fearlessly through the night to terrorize the neighborhood.

The idea came to me just as we reached the end of the street. I lifted up my werewolf head and peered out from under the fangs at the others. "We've been to all the houses on this street. Let's cut through the coulee to the golf course."

It made me laugh, the way everyone stopped short. Like I'd just dared them to break into a house or something. The whole gang was there — the Crow was Brad Reidon, Frankenstein was Ryan Cooper, Count Dracula was Tyler Forster and the Headless Horseman was Eric Sieward. Josh was dressed as Cap'n Hook. And Ringo, of course. Ringo looked crazy enough to go as himself on Halloween.

Everyone stood there staring at me, capes flying behind them.

"You think that's a good idea?" said Josh. His pirate sword dragged on the ground beside him.

"Why not?" I said. "It's shorter than following the road all the way around. We can be down on the golf course in a few minutes. Bet hardly anybody has been to the houses down there. They'll be giving out handfuls at a time."

"Yeah," said Ryan. His voice was hollow behind his rubber Frankenstein mask. "And we could grab a few flagsticks on the way back. I don't think they've taken them down for the winter yet."

Ryan usually went along with anything. He had a whole collection of street signs, lawn ornaments and direction signs. He told his parents they were second-hand, left over after new ones were put up, but he'd swiped most of them.

Brad and Tyler only needed a little shove. Eric would be willing, too. "Look." I pointed. "The moon is coming out. There'll be lots of light. And Josh and I know this coulee like our own back yards."

We all looked up. The last bit of cloud blew across the almost full moon.

"Okay then," said Brad.

We lifted our Halloween sacks, already heavy with candy, and slung them over our shoulders. Except Josh. It was just like him to hang back. Maybe because he'd already seen what happened when I got one of my ideas.

"I don't know, Darien," he said. "It's rough and there's no path except the animal trails. Someone could get hurt."

I figured Josh would go along eventually. He was the new kid and wouldn't want the others to think he was scared. But just to make sure, I hooked him with a lure I knew he wouldn't be able to resist. "We'll be careful, Josh. I want you to come along. It wouldn't be any fun without you."

He gave me one of his "tell me another one" stares, but trudged after the rest of us. We stopped at the coulee edge where the field turned to nothing.

Ringo started acting weird. He jumped over onto the steep slope below and looked up at us, barking furiously. "Be quiet, Ringo!" I said. He whined but did what he was told.

All six of us peered down. It was almost totally black while another cloud passed over the moon. Then the coulee began to shimmer.

Standing there, the wind was at our backs. It whipped our capes around our legs. The long wolf hair on my mask blew out in front of me, across my eyes and mouth. Then the wind pushed us forward. We let out a loud whoop, dropped over the edge and scrambled down the steep slope.

CHAPTER TWENTY

We slid down the upper slope to a deer track that cut across the hill. Brad skidded and landed on his seat, hard. "Ouch! There's cactus all over the place."

I pulled him up. "Then don't be so clumsy."

We kept going, picking our way along the narrow trail. Ringo ran on ahead, yelping like crazy. He took off suddenly, disappearing into the night.

"Ringo," I called. "Come back here!"

He appeared out of the darkness and

stayed close, running back and forth beside us.

I had never been in the coulee at night before. It wasn't the same place. The crisp night air made everything seem bigger, even sound bigger. There were no more clouds now and the moon was bright. It turned the deep coulee into a land of silent shifting shadows and cold silvery light. Buffaloberry and wolf willow branches stretched shadow talons across our path. A thin line, gleaming at the bottom, showed where the creek was. It cut through the tangle of thorny bushes. In the dark shadows, it looked as if the bushes were growing out of the black mouth of the overturned wagon. I could see the dark outline of the upside-down wagon wheels standing in the air and just make out the twisted growth of clematis vines clinging to the rotting spokes.

We made our way down to the creek and around the clump of bushes. The coulee slopes towered above us on both sides. The only sound was the wind howling over our heads. Down here, the gale reached in just far enough to make the dead grasses dip and sigh.

Behind me, Brad stumbled forward but managed to catch himself with a hand against the slope. He stopped to kick whatever it was he had tripped on. "What's this?"

I came up close to him and looked. "What's left of a dead deer. A fawn. It's been here all summer. Just a few bones now."

No one said anything. I took a deep breath. I could feel the night air fill my lungs and move into my blood, making me strong. Like always, I felt stronger, more powerful, here in the coulees.

The six of us made our way along the bottom in silence. We were just going around the first corner when I felt it. Something tugged at me, pulling me back with a jerk.

"Hey!" I protested and turned around to give whoever it was an earful. But my friends were still working their way around a rock. No one was close enough to have touched me.

What was going on? I looked around

again. Nothing was moving. I felt a coolness on my face and a small warning tickle start to itch at the back of my mind. I remembered the shove that had pushed me away from the rattlesnakes.

The others caught up. Ringo stopped barking and sat on the path ahead like he was guarding it, growling deep in his throat. Stupid dog, I thought. But then suddenly his growl grew louder. He stood on all fours and snarled at something behind us.

I looked back at the ridge we had climbed down. A shape stood black against the night sky. Its head was pointed down, as if watching us below. The others saw it, too.

"What is it?" asked Josh. Then his eyes widened. "Your coyote?" he whispered. I was the only one who heard him. I nodded.

"I bet it's a wolf," said Eric.

We moved a little closer to each other. I took a step back up the hill toward the shape. It was looking at me, I knew.

"It's a coyote. A big one," I said. Suddenly it didn't seem like such a good idea to be down there.

"What's the hold-up? A coyote isn't going to bother us. Let's go!" Brad shouldered his sack of candy. "I want to fill this sack with something else besides cactus thorns."

We moved on again, but I lagged behind now. I wanted to see what the coyote would do. Ringo stayed beside me, growling and then whining. The coulee opened up into the valley. Just ahead was the narrow line of woods that bordered the river. The empty, grassy lawn of the fifth fairway stretched between the trees and the row of house lights.

I glanced back one more time. I was the only one to see the shape glide over the edge, almost exactly where we'd climbed down earlier. I waited, but it disappeared into the shadows.

I hurried on. I had to catch the others and get everybody away from the woods and up by the houses. A coyote would not be following people unless something was very wrong. A coyote wouldn't even be alone without other coyotes unless something was wrong.

But when I climbed out of the little gully that ended on the golf course, no one else was there.

CHAPTER TWENTY ONE

For a minute I couldn't breathe. I stared ahead into the shadows, trying to make out any movement in the woods. There was only the wind. Down here, it came whistling through the valley with the river. It whirled through and around the trees, snatching the leaves from their branches. The woods sighed with a constant low moan.

Something grabbed my sleeve. I jumped.

"Are you okay?" asked Josh. I gulped and managed to nod.

"I waited for you. Everyone else thought it would be funny to run ahead and give you a scare. But . . ." He stopped and looked at my eyes. I knew they were wild. I could feel them darting back and forth between him and the shadows.

"What is it? What's the matter, Darien?"

"The coyote. It's following us."

"What?"

"I saw it."

"A coyote isn't going to hurt us."

"This one's different. This one is from my dream."

"Darien . . ." Josh's voice was shaking.

"I know it, Josh!"

There was a low growl from Ringo. We looked around. The coyote stood at the edge of the woods. Watching.

It was close now. Close enough for me to see how big an animal it really was. It was panting hard, eager for something. But it stood motionless, its eyes on fire.

"Come on." I grabbed Josh's arm. "We've got to catch the others. Maybe with all of us together . . ."

We ran then, not daring to look back. The wind pushed us along. Somewhere in the woods an owl hooted, but the sound was whipped away by the wind almost as soon as it reached us. My eyes searched the shadows ahead while my heart pounded in the back of my throat. We were halfway down the fairway before I spotted four crouched shadows scrambling across the grass and into the last few bushes that framed the fifth green. We kept running.

Then I realized Ringo wasn't with us any longer. I turned back, calling for him. I could hear his frantic bark coming at me on the wind.

"Come on, boy!" I yelled as hard as I could. The wind grabbed the words out of my mouth. "Stupid dog," I muttered. We couldn't go back. I blinked hard to clear the tears blurring my eyes.

"Darien. Come on." Josh pulled at me.

We ran across the fairway and the green and through the gap in the bushes where we had seen the shadows disappear. We ran right into an ambush. Bodies sprang out at us from all directions. Shrieks and screams of triumph rang in the clear night. A shadow fell from a low hanging tree branch with a whoop, landing right on top of me. I dropped to my knees.

"Gotcha!" shouted Brad.

Josh pushed him off, yelling, but someone shoved Josh over on top of me. We both sprawled on the ground.

"Stop it!" I screamed. "We've got to get out of here!"

Josh took a deep breath and puckered his mouth. He let loose a piercing shriek of a whistle that rang in my ear. Everyone stopped.

It was too late. A sound, low and menacing, came floating from the shadow of the trees. We all turned and froze. My nightmare came crashing into the real world.

A deep, warning growl rumbled out of the dark shape of the coyote. Before anyone could move or call out, it leaped forward. One, two, three great bounds and it was on us. Snarling and snapping. White froth spewing out of its mouth.

It happened in slow motion. Like those dreams where you run and run and never get anywhere. A raking claw sliced across Brad's face. One long slow ripping arc. He fell, screaming. Tyler, Eric and Ryan scrambled to their feet and fled.

The coyote ignored them. It came straight at me and Josh where we lay sprawled on the ground.

And then the coyote was on top of Josh. Bared fangs gripped the side of his neck. Blood and drool ran together. I gagged from the hot smell. And I watched as the black shape, the moon filling the sky above it, pulled Josh off me.

The next second Ringo came leaping across the green and launched himself at the coyote, snapping and grappling for a hold. The coyote let go of Josh and turned its attention to my dog. Josh lay where he fell, face down in the grass, not moving. A sharp pain shot through me, left me gasping for breath. The coyote threw Ringo off with a furious contortion and for just a moment, the two animals stood facing each other. I could see the coyote gather itself, coiled muscles preparing to attack. There was so much power in its frenzy I wanted desperately to turn away, to spare myself the sight of Ringo getting torn apart.

But I did watch. That was all I could do for my dog. And I saw. As the two animals stood facing each other, the one coiled for attack and the other braced to defend, the night air began first to shimmer, then crack and sparkle in bursts of energy. I felt the barest touch of the presence I knew so well flow over me before it changed into something else, full of power and radiance. It gathered itself into a stream of crackling, spitting air, a charged current that blazed suddenly into a flaming torrent, higher and higher and higher, until the torrent swept down through the night and swirled, spiralled, straight at the coyote.

A brilliant flash blinded me. When I could see again, the stream of flaming air had dimmed and shrunk, leaving only a faint shimmering as if heat waves, impossibly, hovered in the night air. The coyote was gone.

I stumbled, weeping, to where Josh lay

sprawled on the ground. He didn't move when I touched him. I could see the pool of blood collecting under his shoulder. I felt Ringo's breath on my face and heard him whine pitifully. He leaned down and started to lick Josh's face. Ringo's neck and shoulder were a mass of sticky dark fur.

I heard voices shouting a long way off. The shimmering in the air gathered again, this time into a softly glowing cloud that settled over Josh and me for a second before blowing away in the wind. Everything started to spin. The world went black.

CHAPTER TWENTY TWO

I woke the next morning in a strange bed in a strange room. My heart skipped then began to beat furiously. I gulped and waited until my head cleared and my heart slowed down, and then I looked around. A hospital. Mom was sitting in a chair beside my bed, asleep.

The scene from the night before came flooding back. Josh. The coyote. Josh was dead. Then the building panic started to fade, replaced by the memory of a gentle glowing touch, the last thing I remembered.

I pulled the covers tight around me, trembling. The door opened a crack, and Dad appeared. Mom heard him come in and woke up. As soon as she saw I was awake, Mom came over, sat down and wrapped her arms around me. I couldn't stop shaking and then I couldn't stop the sobs that came in great rasping heaves.

It was a long time before Mom's murmured words got through to me. "It's okay, Darien. Everyone's okay."

I looked at her, my eyes stinging. I searched Dad's face, where he stood behind her. I managed a whispered, "Josh."

"He's okay for now, Darien."

A wave broke inside me and retreated, leaving my body scrubbed clean. I collapsed back on the pillow. Mom reached over and pushed the hair back from my forehead. Her hands felt cool and soft.

"What happened? I don't remember getting here or what happened to everybody." I looked around. "Where's Ringo?"

Mom and Dad looked at each other, and then looked at me. "Ringo is at the vet's getting patched up. You don't remember?" said Dad.

"No." It was true. A snarling shape that blocked the sky and reached for Josh filled my mind. "Tell me."

Dad sat down on the bed beside Mom. "What do you remember?"

I closed my eyes. When I finally answered, I looked straight at him. It was time to quit lying. "We were trick-or-treating and decided to go down to the valley bottom. It was my idea. I talked everyone into it."

I paused and swallowed. My mouth was dry. "There was this coyote. It followed us through the coulee. We tried to run back to the houses but —." I stopped, then finished in a rush. "The coyote knocked Brad over and jumped on Josh. Ringo fought it. I guess I passed out or something." The only thing I left out was the blazing air. That part, I knew, was my own, must be my own.

Dad nodded. "The others ran to get help and when they got back, the coyote was gone. They took you, Josh and Brad to the hospital, Darien. Brad will be okay, but his face and shoulder have been clawed quite badly."

Dad stopped and sighed. "Josh is in pretty rough shape. They don't know yet if he'll make it."

My mouth was dry and I couldn't stop my voice from cracking. "What do you mean, they don't know if he'll make it?"

"He lost a lot of blood. He just came out of the operating room and is in recovery. The doctors are watching him."

Josh had waited for me, tried to help me. The coyote had been after me, and Josh just happened to be in the way. And now he might die. I turned my head away, into my pillow.

"There wasn't anything you could do, Darien. You couldn't have known about the coyote."

I heard the words. They were the same ones Mom and Dad used when Jeri died.

But this time they were wrong. I could have done something. I could have stayed away from the coulee. Because I did know about the coyote. My dreams had told me. And I'd seen it.

"You get some rest now, Darien. We'll let you know as soon as we hear anything about Josh. The doctor will be in to check on you in a little while."

I was glad when they left, so I could be alone to let the hot tears run down my cheeks.

I've lost them both, I thought. My little brother, and now my best friend. For the first time I realized that's what Josh was. A friend who'd been there for me even when I didn't know I needed him. I knew better now. But it might be too late.

My insides were writhing like a snake. I kept hearing the words, "No one could do anything," over and over again in my head.

CHAPTER TWENTY THREE

The doctor stopped by later that day with Mom and Dad. They were grinning and the first thing Dad said was, "Josh is going to be okay."

The doctor looked me over and gave me a shot he said was a precaution against something. I was too relieved that Josh was okay to pay much attention. The doctor declared me fit enough to go home. I asked him if I could see Josh and he smiled. "He's been asking for you, actually. You can talk to him for a few minutes, but not too long. He needs to sleep."

While Mom and Dad talked with the doctor outside, I got dressed in the jeans and t-shirt Mom had brought for me. When I went to the bathroom to wash up, I noticed my werewolf costume lying crumpled on the floor under a chair. It was torn. There were dead leaves, grass and dirt smeared on it. I reached over and touched a dark patch on the shoulder. It was still damp and sticky.

When I tapped on Josh's door and peeked in, Josh's parents were in the room with him. They looked at me and I waited for them to send me away, to tell me they didn't want me around Josh. But they didn't. Mrs. Michels actually got up and hugged me.

"We're glad you're okay, Darien," she said.

"I . . . I just wanted to see how Josh was doing."

"He's going to be fine. You go on and say hi and we'll wait outside." They got up and headed for the door. I wanted to tell them what Josh had done, how brave he'd been, how he believed in me. The words didn't come.

Chapter Twenty Three

"He . . . he saved my life, you know," I stammered. "I owe him a lot."

Mr. Michels put his hand on my shoulder and smiled at me. "You're a good friend, Darien. That *is* a lot."

I kept staring at the shut door after they left.

"Hey. I thought you came to see me." Josh's voice was hoarse. I walked over to the bed and looked at him. He was hooked up to an IV, and there were bandages around his shoulder and neck that the hospital gown didn't cover. His face and neck were an angry purple color with red welts, and he looked tired. He couldn't turn his neck. I could see he was hurting, but he smiled at me.

"Remind me not to go trick-or-treating with you again."

"Josh, I'm sorry. I was so dumb."

"Hey, I was teasing. It's not your fault."

"Yeah, it is. The coyote. It was after me and you ..." I stumbled around for words.

He looked at me, a puzzled expression on his face. "What are you talking about? The coyote was mad, as in *loco*. At least that's what everyone tells me. It had rabies. They're giving me a vaccine series to keep me from getting sick. You and Brad, too."

"What are you talking about?" I was confused.

"Didn't anyone tell you? They found the coyote, dead. The rabies is what made it act so weird. It was dying."

I stared at him. "Rabies?" Then I remembered the shot the doctor gave me.

"If anything, we should be thanking Ringo for fighting it off. For such a small guy that dog of yours can really kick butt, eh? How is he doing? I think I owe him a lifetime supply of kibbles."

"He's at the vet's. We're going to go see him after we leave here."

"I hope he's okay, Darien."

"Me too." I sat down on the bed. "I thought . . . it was my dream. But it wasn't. I'm not being haunted."

Josh's smile faded. "Yeah, you are. By yourself."

Neither of us said anything for a long

time. I wasn't going to tell him what'd really killed the coyote. He wouldn't believe me. No one else would either. As long as I knew the truth, it didn't matter. And he was right about the rest, about letting all the anger inside me take over.

"Yeah, I know. It's hard, though."

"Yeah."

"You still saved my life, Josh. You stayed with me. If you hadn't, the coyote would have got me instead."

He smiled again. "In some cultures that would make you my lifelong companion."

"No question." It was my turn to grin.

The door opened and a nurse came in and told me it was time to leave. I told Josh I'd come by the next day, and then let her hustle me out the door.

We stopped to see Brad on the way out, too. He was sleeping, so Mom and Dad went to talk to his parents in the waiting room. I stayed with Brad. One side of his face and shoulder were wrapped in bandages. He woke up while I was standing there.

"You okay?" I asked.

He started to smile and then grimaced. "As long as I don't laugh too much. I've got stitches in my face."

"Do they hurt?"

"Not too bad. I think they gave me something, though, for the pain." He shrugged. "I can handle it. What about Josh, the others?"

"Josh is going to be okay, too. Everyone is. You know about the coyote having rabies?"

"Yeah. They told me I have to have some kind of vaccine shots."

"I'm really sorry, Brad."

"You didn't know. Why should you be sorry?"

"I just feel like if I hadn't talked everyone into going down, none of this would have happened."

"Like I said, you didn't know. Forget it, will you?"

I smiled. "Okay. But it's not just that. After Jeri died, you know . . . I haven't been . . ."

He shrugged. "Are you okay now?"

"I think so. At least, I want to be."

"Alright then."

It was alright then.

CHAPTER TWENTY FOUR

I knew as soon as I walked into the vet's that Ringo was okay. He jumped up in his pen and barked a welcome. Even though he was limping when he trotted over to me, and I could see the fresh welts across his shoulder, he was okay.

"What happens to him now?" I asked the vet.

"We'll have to watch him for a while. He's been vaccinated and I've given him another shot. He should be fine before long.

"Thanks, Ringo," I murmured into his furry neck. He just licked my face.

By the time we got home, it was late afternoon and I was tired. As soon as we finished dinner, I went to bed. Mom and Dad both came up to say good night. Dad closed the window tight, but it still didn't keep out the wind that was starting to pick up again.

Mom came over and smoothed my hair back. I didn't pull away.

"You've had quite a time. Are you sure you're okay?"

"I'm fine, Mom. Just wiped." They were on their way out when something occurred to me.

"Uh, Mom? Dad?" I asked. "Maybe tomorrow, maybe we should pack up Jeri's room."

They both smiled. Mom answered, "We can do that."

Even though I was tired, I couldn't get to sleep for a long time. The wind blowing against the house kept taking me back to the night before and the fiery air that blazed to save us. It already felt years away. I remembered all the other times I'd felt something with me, beside me — the unnaturally soft landing when I was thrown off my bike, the warning pull away from the rattlers, even the slow fall from the tree. It all fit.

And I knew Jeri was gone now. I didn't need him to be there anymore. The knot in my stomach was gone, too.

I did see Jeri once more though — when I finally fell asleep.

My dream started out the same as always. Me and Jeri and Ringo running, laughing, across the prairie. The wind was blowing hard, emptying its breath across the prairies in a hugh sigh.

Instead of the skeleton outfits, Jeri was in his Cookie Monster costume and I was in my werewolf suit. It was crazy, but there we were, howling with Ringo at the full moon hanging above the coulees, staring down on us. Waiting. Watching.

We stopped at the edge of the coulee, laughing hysterically, to catch our breath. Ringo danced in circles around us. Then, just like that, he stopped and looked across the coulee to the ridge on the other side. His ears went straight up and the hair on the back of his neck bristled. He growled deep in his throat. I turned in the direction he was looking and felt the hair on the back of my own neck stand on end.

Suddenly the night was filled with a bizarre howling.

I stared at the dark shape standing on the ridge, boldly black against the moon. The shape lifted a pointed nose to the sky and a wail of tormented fury slashed at us through the night air.

"It's time to go, Dari." The voice at my side was quiet, weary.

I turned to look at my little brother, Jeremiah, blue eyes in a blue painted face. Then I took off my wolf's head and dropped it on the ground. I held both his hands and knelt in front of him so I could look into his face.

"Please, Dari. I'm tired. I want to go now."

"I'll miss you. Thanks for being my brother."

He smiled at me. "We can't let it scare us, huh, Darien?"

"No way," I whispered. Then the hands I

was holding started to glow and soon Jeri was glowing softly all over until I couldn't see him anymore, just a shimmering glitter in the air, a million tiny silver stars that drifted into the night sky.

I looked at the black shape across the coulee for a long time. I didn't turn away until the shape faded and disappeared, too. Then I turned and walked back home.

The wind blew quieter now. It was a warm wind with just a breath of peanut butter and toothpaste.

EPILOGUE

I knew I wouldn't see the coyote again and I didn't. I only saw real ones, sometimes, in the fields during the day. Or I heard them howling in packs at night. But they didn't frighten me anymore.

Jeri's ghost was gone too. It wasn't in his room when Mom and Dad and I packed up his things the next day. I kept the soccer jersey, put it away in my dresser. His ghost wasn't in the coulees either, when me, Josh and Brad and the rest of my friends went hiking or tobogganing on the slopes that winter.

One clear cold day after it snowed, the whole gang went tobogganing before the next chinook could blow through and melt everything. The sun was shining, so it felt warm even though the temperature was below freezing. Snow crystals floated in the sunshine like silver glitter pouring from the sky.

We all took turns on Josh's wooden toboggan or else used crazy carpets. Ringo chased us down the hill, yapping and going so fast he usually ended up somersaulting most of the way down. He just picked himself up and kept on going. Brad brought a snowboard that we all tried. There were a lot of face plants in the snow until we got the hang of it.

There was one slope where, if the three of us went together on the wooden toboggan, we could slide right through the fairway, over the mounds on the other side and into someone's back yard. We had to tumble off to keep from hitting the back of the house.

Afterwards, everyone trooped back to my place to warm up. Mom was ready for us.

Marshmallows were melting in the hot chocolate, and the peanut butter cookies were warm from the oven. The whole kitchen smelled like peanut butter. I laughed out loud. I knew Jeri would.